SERBIAN FAIRY TALES

First compiled by Vuk Stefanović Karadžić

Selected, translated and introduced by Jelena Ćurčić

Illustrated by Rosanna Morris
Edited by Sam Quinn
Assistant Editor Paul Garayo

With generous support from

LOTTERY FUNDED

Supported using public funding by
ARTS COUNCIL ENGLAND

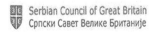

Serbian Council of Great Britain
Српски Савет Велике Британије

2 4 6 8 10 9 7 5 3 1

First published in 2013
by Flying Fish Publications, London

ISBN 978-0-9575250-0-9

Flying Fish Publications is an imprint of Flying Fish Theatriks Ltd
Studio 314 - 315, Cable St Studios
566 Cable Street, London E1W 3HB, UK
Reg. No. 06745197
www.flying-fish.org
publications@flying-fish.org

A catalogue record of this book is available from the British Library

Book design by Paul Garayo
paul.garayo@gmail.com

Printed and bound in Great Britain by
Aldgate Press, London, E1 7RQ

For my father,
Slobodan Manojlov Ćurčić
(1950- 2011)

For all those who have gone before us
and for all those who are yet to come

CONTENTS

INTRODUCTION

Hello, dear reader. The book you hold in your hands is part of the Serbian Fairy Tales project, inspired by the 2012 bicentenary of the first publication of Grimm's Fairy Tales, the opportunity that storytelling affords to link British and world cultures and the proximity of the London Cultural Olympiad. The project was conceived as an international collaboration that crosses time, culture and art form and includes, besides this illustrated book, performance storytelling with music (for adult audiences), on-line content (www.serbianfairytales.com) and a series of Storytelling and Illustration workshops (for children and young people). The project is supported by Arts Council England and Serbian Council of Great Britain.

By 'uncovering the hidden treasures of European folk literature', the project, as a whole, has several main aims: one of these being to introduce Serbian culture, language and literature (which is currently under-represented in English)—not only to the second and third generations of Serbian immigrants living in the UK, but also to a wider audience—in an interesting and innovative way. Furthermore, it aims to present and promote the unique, traditional, ethnic heritage and cultural legacy of the Balkans and to celebrate and enhance British Serb identity.

However, above and beyond introducing the Serbian storytelling tradition or anything relating to the specific, Serbian context, a key aim of the project has been this: to show, through storytelling, how deep down, on the level of myth and legend, fairy tales and folklore—which many (if not all) cultures have at their foundation and which form an integral part of their heritage—there exists a common humanity, a shared universal experience as, for example, Joseph Campbell[1] believes (see Bibliography). All our stories, no matter where we come from, share the same core elements, albeit presented in culture-specific outer form: all our heroes, time and again, are called to adventure, follow a quest, face dangers, are presented with moral choices, receive boons and supernatural aid, become worthy of eternal love. Dragons of some kind or another are always there; so are the ways to defeat them. This reappearance of certain themes and motifs in different mythologies has prompted folklorists such as Antti Amatus

Aarne and, later, Stith Thompson to create a system of classification—the famous Aarne-Thompson tale type index[2, 3] (see Bibliography).

In terms of its scope and import, this project is a UK first. As such, it is an attempt; an attempt at presenting unique material in a unique way. It arose from an artistic need and represents my individual artistic sensibilities. As such, neither the selection nor the translation are definitive; rather, it is my own, personal take at representing my cultural heritage.

The definition of my personal cultural heritage is, however, different to that of my ethnic heritage. This, I feel, calls for further explanation. I come from a land that was, once upon a time. Yugoslavia, the country I was born and grew up in, was a made-up country that existed, in varying form, for less than a century. Like many lands of yore, it was a beautiful country: its realm spanning the magnificent Julian Alps in the North-West, the ancient lake Ohrid in the South, the blue Danube river in the North, the Balkan Mountains in the East and the stunning Adriatic Sea in the West. In the first instance a Kingdom (1918–1943), in the second a flawed attempt at Socialist Utopia (1943–1991), its peoples were as diverse as its stunning landscape and included Serbs, Croats, Slovenes, Bosnians, Macedonians, Montenegrins (all had their own official, autonomous republic within the Socialist Federal Republic of Yugoslavia) and many other regional ethnic minorities. These peoples lived throughout the region, rather than solely in their official areas, i.e. one's ethnicity mattered little in terms of one's choice of a particular part of the land to settle in and call home. Then the wars came. The last decade of the 20th century saw the complete break up of the country through one of the most atrocious conflicts Europe has ever seen. But that is a subject matter for an altogether different book. The reason I mention all this here is to establish the geographical and cultural span covered by the tales contained in this book, but also as an attempt at establishing, and coming to terms with, my own identity: after eleven years of living and working in the UK, I remain Serbian by ethnic origin, Yugoslav by country of origin and personal history—a notion that neither makes me feel particularly proud nor in any way ashamed, individually, as a person and a human being, since none of us have a choice of country, place or family we are born into. I am, however, both delighted with and proud of this cultural heritage, a heritage that shows an inquisitive and imaginative mind of the ordinary people since the beginnings of their tribal history.

This introduces and further clarifies my personal reasons for initiating and realising a project such as this. I had the fortune to be born into a wonderful family, some members of which are no longer among us; in some way, I understand now, this project is my offering to the dead; my close ones, but also my ancestors from thousands of years ago. By continuing to draw attention to the oral tradition of the ordinary people and by presenting it to a large number of diverse communities in English, a language which has become one of the most widely spoken languages in the world, it ensures, in a way, the survival of the race, and of the family.

Serbian Storytelling Tradition: The origins

Serbian storytelling tradition is among the oldest and richest in Europe. Settling in the Balkans in the 6th and 7th century during the period of the Great Migration of the European peoples, Serbs brought with them their pagan gods, rituals and beliefs to see them through their long journey from the East. Like any other society at the time, they lived in a highly symbolic world, with no wall separating the magic from the 'reality'—if they heard thunder, it was God speaking to them (Perun); when they roamed the mountains, they had to tread carefully for they were in the realm of Vilas (forest nymphs); their watermills were meeting places of Vampires (were-wolves); when they looked to the fire, a deity was there, too (Svarog, or Svarožić). Although the introduction and adoption of Christianity as the state religion in the 9th century saw the pagan polytheism pushed aside forcibly in an attempt to have it uprooted for good, old myths remained strong, especially among the rural population. While the peasants accepted baptism and Christ, they saw Christianity as an addition to old Slavic mythology, rather than a replacement of it. They continued to perform ancient rites and kept the mythological view of the world, even when the ancient deities and myths on which those rites were based were all but forgotten, having been replaced by new saints and martyrs. Thus, a specific type of Christianity arose, where old rites and cults of old deities merged with new holidays and saints (as everything else that originated before and after in the Balkans, that melting pot of Europe, the crossroads where peoples and cultures and traditions meet, fall in love and give birth to new and unique forms). Slavic mythology in general, however, has been notoriously difficult to reconstruct with any certainty; the existing evidence being scarce, with almost no written records whatsoever and with many supposed modern discoveries which turned out to be forgeries (or, at the very least, of disputable validity), thrown into the mix (*The Book of Veles*, for example). Echoes of the old mythological beliefs and pagan festivals survive up to this day in folk customs, songs and stories of not only Serbs, but all Slavic nations, thus forming the richest resource for reconstructing the ancient pagan beliefs (although their original mythology and sanctity has, by now, largely been lost).

Serbian folk tales, fables and fairy tales developed from this mythology, sometimes arising from myth, at other times being woven into the body of a myth and adapted to it. Over time, new elements and themes were added; sometimes from other nations and traditions, brought by travellers and learned people, at other times as a reflection on the development or a particular state of the Serbian society itself. They were passed down orally from generation to generation, from mothers and fathers who heard them from their parents and grandparents and great-grandparents, at long winter evenings around the fire when shadows danced and wind and wolves howled outside; at gatherings, during harvest times, when women sat in a circle knitting and spinning the yarn, literally; shepherds told them to each other, as did travellers, fishermen, soldiers—to pass the time and make their work or journeys more pleasant: all the way down to the early nineteenth century when they were finally recorded in print by Vuk Stefanović Karadžić.

Vuk Stefanović Karadžić
[Vook Ste'pha-no-vitch 'Ka-rad-jitch], /ʋûːk stefǎːnoʋite kâradʒite/

(born Nov. 6, 1787, Tršić, Serbia, (then in the Ottoman Empire)—died Feb. 6, 1864,Vienna, Austria)

Vuk was a philologist and linguist, 'the father of the study of Serbian folklore' and the major reformer of the Serbian language. His personal story is wondrous. As Meša Selimović observes, in his study entitled *For and Against Vuk*[4] (see Bibliography) there was something strange, adventurous, brave and daring in Karadžić's decision to move away from his modest origins to the European centre of scholarly research at the time, Vienna, and to attempt to make a living out of writing. He learnt to read and write from his relative, Jevta Savić Čortić, who was the only literate person in the area at the time, then continued his education at the monastery Tronoša; this was short-lived, however, since he was sent to graze the cattle more often than he was given any lessons, so his father brought him back home. In 1804 he attempted to enrol at the Grammar School in Sremski Karlovci but due to his mature age (he was 19 at the time), he was not accepted. Subsequently he became one of the first students of the newly-founded Grande École in Belgrade. He worked as a school teacher, then a scribe to different military leaders and in this position he served his country during the first Serbian uprising against the Ottomans (1804–1813) as, due to illness (a lame leg) he could not take up arms. The uprising failed and Karadžić decided to leave Serbia and go to Vienna, rather than to follow Karađorđe and other leaders to Russia. There he met Jernej Kopitar, an esteemed Slovenian linguist

ix

and philologist, who introduced him to Slavic scholarship and encouraged him to collect poems and folk songs, as well as to write a grammar of the popular Serbian language and a dictionary.

He was well known in Europe and familiar to such giants as Jacob Grimm, Goethe and historian Leopold von Ranke (Karadžić was the primary source for Ranke's *Serbische Revoluzion* (*Serbian Revolution*), written in 1829; Goethe described some of the poems in Karadžić's collections as 'excellent and worthy of comparison with Solomon's *Song of Songs*', and Jacob Grimm was enthralled by them and translated '*The Walled-Up Wife*' poem into German). He was a member of a number of European academies and learned societies, decorated by Russian and Austro-Hungarian monarchs, Prussian King and the Russian Academy of Science. UNESCO has proclaimed 1787 the year of Vuk Karadžić.

Karadžić reformed the Serbian literary language and standardised the Serbian Cyrillic alphabet by following strict phonemic principle devised by the German grammarian and philologist Johann Christoph Adelung: 'Write as you speak and read as it is written.' This reform, however, did not come about all of a sudden; Karadžić had predecessors who attempted to champion the language of the people above the official, church language which was the language of literature and press at the time: Gavril Stefanović Venclović wrote in the vernacular tongue as early as the first decades of the eighteenth century, thus anticipating Karadžić's reform some hundred years before it actually occurred. There were others, too, who helped this process along: Sava Mrkalj, Dositej Obradović, Pavle Solarić, Atanasije Stojković and, to some extent, Lukijan Mušicki, to name but a few.

Vuk Karadžić was the one who brought this long process of language reform to a successful conclusion: he created one of the simplest and most logical spelling systems, establishing that Serbian contains thirty distinct sounds. He disposed of eighteen letters for which the spoken language had no use and intoduced new letters for six sounds which were not previously represented in the Cyrillic alphabet. His proposed reform encountered strong opposition from the church and from writers; however, in 1868 Serbian government finally adopted Karadžić's amended alphabet.

Karadžić travelled extensively across the Balkan region collecting and recording poems and songs, folk tales, fables and fairy tales, customs, riddles and proverbs from Serbia, Bosnia, Herzegovina, Croatia and other areas, thus contributing not only to the field of folk literature but also anthropology and ethnography. His works include:

- *Serbian Folk Poems*, eight volumes in total (1814–1866)
- *Serbian Lexicon*, a Serbian-German-Latin dictionary (1ˢᵗ edition 1818; 2ⁿᵈ expanded edition 1852)
- *Serbian Folk Tales* (1821, 1853, 1870)
- *Serbian Grammar* (1824)
- *The Lives of Prominent Serbian Leaders* (1827)
- *Serbian Proverbs and Customs* (1836)
- *Montenegro and Montenegrins* (1837)
- *A Treasure Chest for History: the Language and Customs of the Serbian People* (1849, 1867)
- *German-Serbian Dictionary* (1972)
  and translation of the New Testament into Serbian (1847)

Vuk and the Brothers Grimm

The rise of Romanticism in 19ᵗʰ century Europe saw a revival of interest in traditional folk tales with the Brothers Grimm at the helm of the new movement, devising and establishing the method of transcribing the tales 'from the mouths of the people'. Vuk Stefanović Karadžić was the Serbian equivalent to the Brothers Grimm. Encouraged by Jacob Grimm himself and spurred on by Jernej Kopitar to persevere in this labour of love, Karadžić travelled far and wide across the region collecting tales. His second collection of folk tales, published in Vienna in 1853, contains a dedication to Jacob Grimm, in the form of a letter (also included here); Grimm was deeply touched by this and wrote back to express his gratitude and enchantment with the 'exquisite tales'.

Karadžić's daughter Mina translated the 2ⁿᵈ collection into German in 1854. Some of the tales from my selection have been translated into English in the past (*Hero Tales and Legends of the Serbians*, Vojislav M. Petrović, London 1914; *Serbian Fairy Tales* by Elodie L. Mijatović, New York Mc Bride 1918). However, the majority of the tales in my selection have never been translated into English until now.

Criteria for my work:
The selection

The preface to the 1853 edition contains Karadžić's own attempt at classification of the tales, into 'male' and 'female', the latter being those tales that 'tell of wonders that cannot be', and which abound with magical animals, mythical heroes and supernatural transformations, and the former being a kind of catalogue of potential destinies of men and women, telling about things that could actually occur and that contain general explanation of life and examination of human predicaments in often comical style (as the best way to teach is through humour). He further admits that there are some tales that belong equally to both categories. This classification is in line with modern folklorists' division of oral tales into 'fairy tales', which take place in a separate 'once-upon-a-time' setting of nowhere-in-particular, and are not intended to be understood as true, and 'legends' which tell of events that have actually occurred, often at a particular time and place (although they too contain elements of the supernatural, this is mainly as a means of driving the action forward and calling for an emotional response from the listener).

As this project focuses on fairy tales, all of the twenty tales selected for this illustrated publication are 'female'. From the mountain of narratives in Karadžić's collections, where some stories have several versions and variants, I have chosen the most characteristic tales to represent these 'types' of fairy tales many of which contain themes, motifs and forumlae present in the folk tales of other nations, though with typically Serbian elements, such as the Aždaja, for example (see The Young Tzarevich and the Aždaja, Note 5). Most of these tales tell of the time when the forests held both a magical enchantment and a foreboding, echoing with the sounds of dangerously beautiful Vilas' singing (see The Maiden Who Was Faster Than a Horse, Note 1), and contain many elements of the aforementioned Slavic pagan mythology, thus distinguishing them from the classic stories of kings of imprecise realms.

As Milan Mihailović points out in the television series *The Mysteries of Serbia*[5] (see Bibliography), at the top of the Serbian mythological pantheon sit two royalties: His Majesty The Zmaj, and Her Majesty The Vila. Many of the tales here are focused around these two characters; others feature Animal Heroes, Witches, Giants or even ordinary folk who, either through some magical intervention or, often, through 'outsmarting' (this seems to be a highly popular theme in Serbian folklore) overcome evil adversaries and rise to glory. In terms of the running order, the tales are not grouped into categories; rather, I have interspersed these different types and attempted to create a sort of a smorgasbord of narratives, believing this to be of greater enjoyment for the reader.

My personal favourite has to be The Bear's Son—a strangely peculiar tale which, although belonging to a type of tale found not only in Europe but also further afield (see Bear's Son, Note 4), is also completely unlike any other folk or fairy tale I have ever heard or read. Starting off in a fairly standard way, then, all of a sudden, half-way through, introducing a rather surreal, highly amusing element reminiscent of *Alice in Wonderland* with its crazy turn of events and entirely arbitrary dimensions, it seems to embody the very nature of storytelling, particularly in its oral form: the fluidity, the freedom and ability to change and become another version of itself, or join up with other stories and become yet a new tale, as long as the tale is being told, a good storyteller will yet find a way to bind it all together. A tall story, indeed! I have a little theory about the origin of this particular version but, rather than stating it here, I have decided to add it as a note at the end of the story, so as not to spoil your enjoyment.

The collection, not by accident, opens with The Maiden Who Was Faster Than a Horse. As a 21ˢᵗ century woman, I enjoy a good old tale where the female character leads the action and has the last laugh, instead of being a passive heroine withering away at the top of some tower waiting to be rescued by some Prince Valiant. The tale is also featured in my storytelling performance for adults which accompanies this book (on tour 2012–2015). The show was performed for London audiences several times prior to the making of this book, and this particular tale has provoked the most comments and questions, as the modern audiences do not seem to find it easy to comprehend a fairy tale where the hero does not get to ride off into the sunset with his lady on the back; I've had to explain that it is the ultimate story of chase and that the fair maiden simply one-ups the men.

The Translation

Translation is a tricky business and, as such, a controversial one. There will be as many translations of any given text as there are translators; it is entirely possible to keep the meaning accurate while presenting it in a variety of tones and styles. I have approached the task of translation of these tales with the intention of remaining faithful to the original transcriptions as much as possible. I strived to reflect the local colour and atmosphere without adding too much (if any) personal touches and embellishment, keeping the stories clearly and unmistakably rooted in the past, both in the ancient pagan past which provides the settings for the stories, and the more recent 19ᵗʰ century past, when the stories were first collected and published. I kept the language simple and close to the spoken language, in a manner which would suggest an ordinary person narrating a tale, rather than a literary creation by an author. At times, this was difficult, as the writer in me wanted to change whole passages in some tales, add more description in others, cut or alter unnecessary repetition, create different endings and so on. In this sense, these truly are translations of the tales, rather than my re-tellings of them. Furthermore, although it was important to ensure that the English language standards were upheld without fail, it was even more important to ensure that the tales did not end up sounding like they were told in the English language in the first place. It is my belief that, in order to understand a culture of a nation, one must first understand its language or, rather, the way a language works, as the way a language works reflects the way a mind thinks. On this note, I must express my eternal gratitude to my wonderful editor Sam Quinn, whose corrections and comments have been invaluable in ensuring the high standard of these translations; but I also must apologise for not always following his advice and for insisting on some choices and turns of phrase. As the final editorial decisions were mine, if anything in these tales sounds somewhat too Serbian and not English enough, than that would be down to me.

Finally, a couple of notes on translation choices: I decided to keep the English variant spelling for words such as Tzar, Tzarevich and Tzaritza, since these titles have already entered the English language through translations of Russian texts; Serbian spelling is added in the end notes. Further, although the title itself (Tzar) had, by 19th century, come to be considered (by Western Europeans) simply as an equivalent to King, I deemed it more appropriate to use the term Tzar (as it is used in the tales), in order to maintain the notion of a Slavic monarch, as opposed to any, undefined monarch.

Some terms have been rather difficult to translate in an easily accessible way, as I am introducing them here for the very first time, such as Brother-with-God, or Sister-with-God. These terms relate to the custom (still common in contemporary Serbian society) whereby a person could name another their brother or sister, as a mark of deep friendship and loyalty. In the past, this practice involved ceremonial mingling of each other's blood (hence the term: blood brothers); nowadays, it is enough to simply say it (and, perhaps, drink to it). The tales in this collection make good use of this term throughout.

Lastly, an explanatory note on some translation choices based on Serbian grammar: Serbian language, like many other Slavic languages and unlike the English language, uses inflection (modification of a word to express different grammatical categories such as tense, grammatical mood, grammatical voice, aspect, person, number, gender and case). Pronouns, nouns, adjectives (and some numerals) decline, i.e. change the word ending to reflect case—grammatical category and function. In Serbian, nouns are declined into 7 cases: nominative, genitive, dative, accusative, vocative, locative and instrumental. Hence, while Aždaja is the nominative case, the vocative case (used for a noun identifying the person—or an animal, or an object—being addressed) changes the word ending to become Aždajo (see The Young Tzarevich and the Aždaja), Mara becomes Maro (see Pepeljuga). In modern English, the nominative case is used for vocative expressions, and is set off from the rest of the sentence with punctuation in writing—commas or exclamation mark, and with pauses as interjections in speech.

The Notes

A great majority of the tales here are accompanied by ample explanatory notes. The notes are located at the end of each story, rather than at the back of the book, for easier accessibility by the reader. I use the notes to point out peculiarities and the diversity of the tales, their narrative personality, as well as to draw comparisons with other storytelling traditions and to draw attention to universal motifs, characters and plots, thus highlighting the cross-cultural influences and transmissions. Most of the notes pertain to folkloric interpretations of flora and fauna, geographical locations, some customs or terms specific to Serbian tradition (e.g. the aforementioned Brother-with-God). However, just as the knowledge and sources for interpretation of Slavic mythology available today are but the tip of the iceberg, these notes are but the tip of the iceberg of the body of Serbian folklore; they are in no way extensive, merely scratching the surface.

Since a relatively high volume of Serbian words is introduced throughout the tales, the notes also include English spelling and International Phonetic Alphabet transcriptions for these words. Appendix 1 at the back of the book contains Serbian alphabet—Cyrillic and Latin.

Finally, in keeping with the project's motto of crossing time, culture and art form, the notes are given from a contemporary perspective and often, where appropriate, include comments relating to modern society, as well as the historic one.

I hope you will enjoy reading these tales as much as I have enjoyed selecting and translating them. And now, let the adventure begin!

Jelena Ćurčić

London, December 2012

Letter to Jacob Grimm (from the preface to the 2nd collection of Serbian Folk Tales, 1853)

'To the renowned German Jacob Grimm

My dear and revered friend,

it is mostly due to yours and the late Kopitar's efforts that the Serbian folk poems and songs have become well known across Europe and other parts of the learned world, to the glory of the Serbian people. Furthermore, back in 1823 when I had the pleasure and the privilege of meeting you in Kassel, you encouraged and advised me to also collect and publish Serbian folk tales: this little book sees that wish fulfilled. I am convinced that this book will please you more than it could please any other soul; therefore I have taken the liberty of adorning it with your esteemed name. I will be particularly pleased and delighted should you find these tales, like you did the poems, to be worthy of the Serbian people.

Vienna, 1852

Your grateful friend,
Vuk Stefanović Karadžić'

The Maiden Who Was Faster Than a Horse

Once upon a time there lived a maiden who was not born from mother and father but made by Vilas[1] out of snow gathered from a bottomless pit[2] under the light of St Ilija's sun[3]. The wind breathed life into her, mountain dew suckled her, the forest dressed her in leaves and the meadow adorned her with flowers. She was whiter than snow, her cheeks rosier than a rose, she was more radiant than the sun; she was such as the world had never seen before nor shall it ever see again. This maiden sent out word that on such and such a day, at such and such a place there was to be a race, and that the young man who could overtake her on his horse would win her for himself. In no time, the word spread across the great wide world, and thousands of suitors on their horses gathered, each one better than the last. The Tzar's[4] son himself came to take part in the race. The maiden stood on her mark and the suitors all lined up on their horses; the maiden in between them with nothing but her legs to carry her. She spoke to them thus:

'I have placed a golden apple[5] at the finish line; the first one amongst you to reach the apple will have me for himself. But if I reach and take the apple before you, you will all drop dead on the spot; so be careful what you do.'

The horsemen exchanged glances, each one of them hoping that he would be the one to win the maiden. They said to each other:

'We know indeed that she will not be able to escape any one of us on foot; one of us will win, the one who has God and luck on his side today.'

So the maiden clapped her hands, and anon they all took off. Half-way there, however, the maiden gained quite an advantage as she sprouted some kind of tiny wings from under her armpits. At this, the horsemen chided each other, and prodded and spurred their horses on, to catch up with the maiden. Seeing this, the maiden plucked a hair from her head, dropped it on the ground and presently a great big forest appeared, so great and so big that the suitors all began to lose their way. They wandered here and there but still followed her track, and although she managed to gain quite an advantage once more, they spurred their horses on and ere long caught up with her again.

When the maiden saw that the forest too had fallen short of stopping the suitors, she shed a single tear—and a tremendous river burst forth, nearly drowning them all. None pursued the maiden any further, bar the Tzar's son himself, who swam through the waters on his horse's back. Seeing the maiden too far ahead he called to her three times in the name of God to stop—and she stopped in her tracks. He then caught her and sat her on the horse behind him and swam back across the river and onto the river bank, taking a road up a mountain, homeward bound. But as he reached the summit of the mountain he turned and looked back—and the maiden was nowhere to be seen.

Notes

1. Vila [**vee**-ler] /ʋǐːla/- Slavic version of nymph. According to Serbian folklore, Vilas dwell in rivers, lakes and ponds, sky and clouds, mountains, caves and other clandestine places. They sometimes appear as swans, horses, falcons, wolves or other animals that they can shape-shift into but usually they appear as beautiful maidens, naked or dressed in white with long flowing hair. Generally, they are benevolent unless provoked, they are just, they help the poor and the disadvantaged, and are a good omen. Woe betide those who anger them, however, for they will perish from a Vila's glance.
It is said that if even one of her hairs is plucked (by a human), a Vila will die, or be forced to change back to her true shape. A human may gain the control of a Vila by stealing feathers from her wings. Once she gets them back, however, she will disappear.
A Vila's voice is as beautiful as the rest of her, and one who hears it loses all thought of food, drink or sleep, at times, for days. Despite their feminine charms, however, Vilas are fierce warriors. When they battle, the earth is said to shake. They have healing and prophetic powers and are sometimes willing to help human beings. At other times they lure young men to dance with them, which according to their mood can be a very good or a very bad thing for the man. They ride on horses or deer when they hunt with their bows and arrows and will kill any man who defies them or breaks his word. Fairy circles of deep thick grass are left where they have danced; these should never be trodden upon, as this brings bad luck.

2. A bottomless pit is a very deep pit in the mountains where the snow never melts and stays throughout the year.

3. St Ilija's (Elijah's) sun is the Summer sun around St Ilija's day, which is celebrated

on 2nd August. According to folklore, St Ilija's sun has a special brightness to it as it stops in the sky three times during the course of the day.

4. Tzar [tsahr], /tsar/ (Serbian: Car) is a title given to a supreme ruler, a monarch equal to emperor in the European Slavic medieval sense of the word.

5. In Serbian folklore, a golden apple is a symbol of wealth and happiness.

The young Tzarevich and the Aždaja

Once upon a time there lived a Tzar who had three sons. One day the eldest one went to hunt in the forest, but as soon as he left the town, a hare[1] jumped out of a bush and the Tzarevich[2] gave chase. He chased up and he chased down, until he chased the hare into a watermill[3]. But when the Tzarevich reached the watermill he found that the hare had turned into an Aždaja[4], and this Aždaja grabbed and devoured him. When several days had passed and the Tzarevich failed to return home, they began to wonder what had happened to him. So the second son went a-hunting, and as soon as he left the town, a hare jumped out of a bush and the Tzarevich gave chase. He chased up and he chased down, until he chased the hare into the same watermill. But as the Tzarevich came to the watermill he found that the hare had turned into an Aždaja, and the Aždaja grabbed and devoured him. When several more days had passed and neither of the two Tzar's sons had returned, the whole of the Tzar's court became dismayed. So the youngest son went a-hunting, hoping to find his brothers. As soon as he left the town, a hare jumped out of a bush and the young Tzarevich gave chase. He chased up and he chased down, until he chased the hare into the watermill. But the young Tzarevich desired not to follow the hare into the mill, and decided instead to go and look for other quarry, saying to himself: 'I'll get you yet, when I'm back'. After that he roamed the mountain for some time looking for game, but as he found nothing, he went back to the watermill. There he found an old woman and greeted her thus:

'God help you, grandma!'

And the old woman replied:

'God help you, my child!'

Then the young Tzarevich asked:

'Grandma, where is my hare?'

To this, the old woman replied:

'That was not a hare, my child, but an Aždaja, that slaughtered and slew many

4

a folk around here.'

The young Tzarevich felt deeply saddened by these words.

'That must be how my two brothers perished then, too', he said. 'What are we to do?'

'Indeed, that is how they perished', was her response. 'But there is nothing to be done; go home, lest you meet the same fate.'

Then the young Tzarevich said:

'You know what, Grandma? I know that you are just as keen as I am to be rid of this pest for good.'

And the old woman agreed:

'O my dear child, of course I am! I am also under its thumb, and there is no escape.'

So the young Tzarevich continued:

'Listen very carefully to what I am about to say to you. When the Aždaja comes back, ask it where it goes and where its strength lies, and then kiss the place where it keeps its strength, pretending you love it so much, and when I come back you will tell me where that is.'

Then the young Tzarevich returned to his father's palace, and the old woman remained in the watermill. When the Aždaja came back, the old woman began to enquire:

'Where on Earth have you been? And whither do you go every day? You never tell me where you go.'

And the Aždaja replied:

'O my dear Grandma, I go far and wide.'

Then the old woman began to fawn on the Aždaja:

'And why do you go so far and so wide? Pray tell me where your great strength lies...For if I knew where your great strength lay, I know not what I would do for joy; I would kiss and kiss that place.'

And the Aždaja laughed heartily and said:

'Over there in that hearth, that's where my strength lies.'

So the old woman leaped over to the hearth and hugged and kissed the hearthstones ardently, and the Aždaja burst out laughing and said:

'Silly old woman, that's not where my strength lies! My strength is in that tree outside the watermill.'

Then the old woman ran over to the tree and hugged and kissed it lovingly, and the Aždaja burst out laughing again and said:

'Leave it, silly old woman, that's not where my strength lies.'

'Well, where is it, then?' she asked.

To this, the Aždaja replied:

'My strength is so, so far away, you could never get there. In a far, far away

Tzardom, there is a lake outside the Tzar's town, and in that lake there is another Aždaja, and in that Aždaja there is a wild boar[5], and in that wild boar there is a hare, and in that hare there is a pigeon, and in that pigeon there is a robin, and in that robin—that's where my strength lies.'

Hearing this, the old woman confessed:

'That, indeed, is very far away; I cannot kiss that place.'

The following day, when the Aždaja had left the watermill, the young Tzarevich came back and the old woman recounted everything the Aždaja had said. So the young Tzarevich went home and put on shepherd's clothes, took a shepherd's staff and thus, disguised as a shepherd, set off on his journey. He went from village to village, from town to town, until he reached the far away Tzardom and the Tzar's town with the nearby lake where the other Aždaja lived. In the town, he enquired with the townsfolk if anybody was in need of a shepherd, and they told him that the Tzar himself needed one. So he went straight to the Tzar's palace and when he was brought to the Tzar, the Tzar asked him if he was truly intending to mind the Tzar's sheep, and he swore that he was. Then the Tzar advised him thus:

'There is a lake nearby, and next to the lake there is a beautiful grazing field. As soon as the sheep are out to graze, they go straight for that field and scatter around the lake, but none of the shepherds that ventured there, ever came back; so I'm telling you, son, not to let the sheep lead you there, but you should lead them where you desire.'

The young Tzarevich thanked the Tzar and went to lead the sheep out to graze, taking with him two hounds fast enough to catch a hare in the field, and a falcon able to catch any bird in the sky, and he also took bagpipes. No sooner had he taken the sheep out of the pen, than he led them straight to the lake, and no sooner had the sheep reached the lake, than they scattered around the lake. The young Tzarevich put the falcon upon a log, and the hounds and the bagpipes on the ground beside the log; then he rolled up his sleeves and the legs of his trousers and stepped into the lake, shouting:

'O Aždajo! O Aždajo! Come out and duel with me, unless you are a woman!'[6]

And the Aždaja replied:

'I'm coming, young Tzarevich, I'm coming!'

Not long after, out came the Aždaja, huge, terrible, horrible! No sooner had the Aždaja come out, than it took on and wrestled the young Tzarevich, and they wrestled till high noon. As the noon sun rose high and burnt bright in the sky, the Aždaja said:

'Will you let me, young Tzarevich, dip my head in the lake, and I'll throw you high up in the sky above the clouds.'

And the young Tzarevich replied:

'O Aždajo, leave your nonsense be; if I were to have a Tzar's daughter kiss me

8

upon the forehead, I would throw you even higher!'

Hearing this, the Aždaja released its grip and slipped back into the depths of the lake. As dusk fell, the young Tzarevich washed and groomed himself nicely, put the falcon upon his shoulder, and the bagpipes under his arm and, with the hounds by his side, led the sheep back to the town, playing the bagpipes all the way. As he reached the town, all the townsfolk gathered and wondered greatly how could it be that this shepherd was able to return from the lake whence none before him had returned.

The next morning the young Tzarevich got ready and took the sheep straight out to graze at the lakeside once more. But this time the Tzar sent two horsemen after him, by stealth, to go and see what it was that he was doing, and the men rode their horses to the summit of a high mountain, the better to see what was going on below. The shepherd, as he reached the lake, put the falcon upon a log, and the hounds and the bagpipes on the ground beside the log; then he rolled up his sleeves and the legs of his trousers and stepped into the lake, shouting:

'O Aždajo! O Aždajo! Come out and duel with me some more, unless you are a woman!'

Sure enough, the Aždaja replied:

'I'm coming, young Tzarevich, I'm coming!'

Not long after, out came the Aždaja, huge, terrible, horrible! No sooner had the Aždaja come out, than it took on and wrestled the young Tzarevich, and they wrestled till high noon. As the noon sun rose high and burnt bright in the sky, the Aždaja said:

'Will you let me, young Tzarevich, dip my head in the lake, and I'll throw you high up in the sky above the clouds.'

And the young Tzarevich replied:

'O Aždajo, leave your nonsense be; if I were to have a Tzar's daughter kiss me upon the forehead, I would throw you even higher!'

Hearing this, the Aždaja released its grip and slipped back into the depths of the lake. As dusk fell, the young Tzarevich did as before and led the sheep back to the town, playing the bagpipes all the way. As he reached the town, all the townsfolk pondered and wondered greatly how could it be this shepherd came home every night when none before him had returned. The two horsemen had reached the Tzar's palace before the young Tzarevich and recounted everything they saw and heard to the Tzar. Now, when the Tzar saw the shepherd return yet again, he summoned his daughter and explained everything he had learned from the horsemen to her, then said:

'On the morrow, you are to go with the shepherd to the lake and to kiss him upon the forehead.'

Hearing this, the Tzar's daughter burst into tears and began to plead with her

11

father:

'You have no-one other than me in this whole wide world, and you don't even care if I perish!'

And her father consoled and encouraged her thus:

'Fear not, my daughter. You yourself know how many shepherds we've had, and each one of them went to the lake and never came back, and this one has been wrestling with the Aždaja for two days now, and not a hair from his head is missing. I have faith that he can overcome this Aždaja; go with him tomorrow, so that we can be rid of this pest that slaughtered and slew so many a folk.'

The next morning as the dawn broke and the sun came out, the shepherd rose and the maiden rose, and they began preparing to go to the lake. The shepherd was happy as a lark, over the moon; the Tzar's daughter sad as a weeping willow, crying her eyes out. So the shepherd consoled her thus:

'Dear sister, I beg you not to cry, just do as I say: when the time comes, run up to me and kiss me upon the forehead, and all shall be well.'

So they set off and led the sheep along the road, the shepherd joyfully playing the bagpipes, while the maiden walked beside him shedding tears; from time to time he would cease playing in order to say to her:

'Cry not, my precious, fear not.'

No sooner had they reached the lake, than the sheep scattered around the lake, and the young Tzarevich put the falcon upon a log, and the hounds and the bagpipes on the ground beside the log; then he rolled up his sleeves and the legs of his trousers and stepped into the lake, shouting:

'O Aždajo! O Aždajo! Come out and duel with me some more, unless you are a woman!'

And the Aždaja replied:

'I'm coming, young Tzarevich, I'm coming!'

Not long after, out came the Aždaja, huge, terrible, horrible! No sooner had the Aždaja come out, than it took on and wrestled the young Tzarevich, and they wrestled till high noon. As the noon sun rose high and burnt bright in the sky, the Aždaja said:

'Will you let me, young Tzarevich, dip my head in the lake, and I'll throw you high up in the sky above the clouds.'

And the young Tzarevich replied:

'O Aždajo, leave your nonsense be; if I were to have a Tzar's daughter kiss me upon the forehead, I would throw you even higher!'

No sooner had he said that, than the Tzar's daughter ran up to him, and kissed him upon the cheek, and upon the eye, and upon the forehead. Then the young Tzarevich picked up and threw the Aždaja high up in the sky above the clouds, and the Aždaja, as it came down and hit the ground, burst to smithereens, and

12

as it burst to smithereens, a wild boar jumped out of it and fled, and the young Tzarevich turned to the hounds:

'Go, get him!'

And the hounds ran after the boar, and caught him and tore him to pieces; but a hare jumped out of the boar and fled, so the young Tzarevich turned to the dogs again:

'Go, get him!'

And the hounds ran after the hare, and caught him and tore him to pieces; but a pigeon fled out of the hare and away, so the young Tzarevich released the falcon, and the falcon caught the pigeon and brought him to the young Tzarevich. The young Tzarevich took the pigeon and cut him open, and inside he found a robin; he held him tight, then said:

'Now tell me where my brothers are.'

'I will, if you do me no harm', the robin replied. 'Right beside your father's town, there is a watermill, and inside the watermill there are three saplings; cut the saplings down, then hit the stump with the cut off twigs; an iron door to a big cellar will open, and in the cellar there are many a folk, young and old, rich and poor, big and small, women and girls, men and boys, so many you could people a whole Tzardom—that's where you will find your brothers, too.'

No sooner had the robin said this, than the young Tzarevich wrung its neck.

The Tzar himself had come out and climbed the summit of the mountain whence the horsemen had observed the shepherd, and he watched and saw it all too. As the shepherd overcame the Aždaja thus, dusk began to fall; he washed and groomed himself nicely, put the falcon upon his shoulder, and the bagpipes under his arm and, with the hounds by his side, led the sheep back to the town, playing the bagpipes all the way, while the maiden walked beside him, still affrighted. As he reached the town, all the townsfolk gathered in wonderment. The Tzar, who had witnessed the young Tzarevich's bravery from the top of the mountain, summoned him then and gave him the hand of his daughter in marriage; presently they were married, and the wedding celebrations lasted a whole week. Then the young Tzarevich revealed his true self and told them who he was and where he had come from, and the Tzar and the whole town rejoiced even more. He then wished to go back to his own home with his new bride, and the Tzar gave them a big cortege to accompany them on their journey.

As they reached the watermill, the young Tzarevich halted the cortege and went inside, cut the saplings, then hit the stump with the cut off twigs and presently the cellar door opened to reveal a great big congregation. Then the young Tzarevich ordered them all to leave, one at a time, as he stood by the door. As the people came out, there came his two brothers; he kissed them and he hugged them. When all the folk had come out, they thanked him for saving them and for releasing them, and went back to their homes. And the young Tzarevich took his brothers and his new bride back to their father's palace, and there he lived and ruled happily ever after.

Notes

1. According to Serbian folklore, a hare is a demonic animal, often an omen of disaster and weather changes. Pregnant women must not eat hare meat, yet it can have restorative powers for the sick. As it sleeps during the day and is active at night, and as it can, just like the Moon, quietly appear and disappear, a hare is a lunar symbol.

2. Tzarevich [**tsah**-re-vitch], /ˈtsarevitɕ/ (Serbian: Carević) is a son of a Tzar; a Prince.

3. A watermill is a structure that uses a water wheel to power a mechanical process of grinding grains into flour. Apart from their importance in providing the daily bread, in Serbian and Slavic mythology watermills hold a special, mythical meaning as the gathering places for spirits and demons during night-time, and Vodenjak [vo-**den**-yahk], /ˌʋodeːɲak/, the water spirit and the lord of water, resides close by in his crystal palace at the bottom of a river or a stream. Anyone who grew up in ex-Yugoslavia during 1970s or 1980s will remember the cult Serbian horror film 'Leptirica' ('The Moth', also know as 'The She-Butterfly', 1973, dir Đorđe Kadijević, adapted from the short story 'Ninety Years Later' by Milovan Glišić, published in 1880–1917, years before Bram Stoker's 'Dracula'), and the cursed watermill possessed by the most famous Serbian vampire, Sava Savanović.

4. In Serbian and South Slavic mythology, there is a differentiation between two types of dragon-like creatures: Zmaj [zmahy] /zmai/ and Aždaja [azh-**dah**-ya] /ˌaʒˈdaːja/. Whilst Zmaj can be good or bad, a man's ally or foe, and is generally respected as a creature of extraordinary strength and a worthy opponent, Aždaja is a being of pure evil. It is a mythical creature resembling a huge winged snake or a lizard, often with three or nine heads, four stumpy legs and bat-like wings. It lives in hostile and dark places, spits blue fire and creates an infernal racket with its terrible shrieks; it is voracious and ferocious. It is believed that an Aždaja comes into being when a snake keeps devouring other snakes and then grows wings and legs one hundred years later (e.g. the famous Christian icon is described in Serbian as 'St George slaying the Aždaja', not a Zmaj).

5. According to Serbian folklore, wild boar is a demonic creature. It is a symbol of strength, rashness, forcefulness and foolishness.

6. This does not mean that women are cowardly; simply that women are not to be fought with physically, but protected and cared for instead. A man who raises his hand at a woman is considered to be cowardly and dishonourable.

The Old Man Who Outsmarted the Giants

Once upon a time there lived an old man who was a miller. This miller had lots of young children, and he lived with his children in his watermill. One evening, a Giant[1] appeared out of nowhere, and went straight for the mill. He bid good evening and God's help to the old man, and asked him if he could stay the night there. The old man offered him lodgings for the night; but the Giant was intent on killing the old man and on taking over his mill. He stayed the night there and in the morning, the old man said to the Giant:

'So, you had your lodgings for the night, now God help thee and fare thee well.'

But the Giant replied:

'Whichever one of us is stronger shall remain as the Lord of this place.'

'All right then, if that is what you wish', said the old man. 'I have nothing to fear.'

Then the Giant challenged him to a wrestle, but the old man responded thus:

'Hm, that is nothing for me, we shall not wrestle, we shall instead pick up a stone each and squeeze it in our hands until the water comes running out of it.'

The Giant accepted this wager, grabbed a great, big stone and squeezed it so hard it crumbled to dust, but not a drop of water came out of it. Then the old man, pretending to take a stone, grasped a lump of fresh, mild, white cheese, squeezed it and, lo and behold, water came running out. The Giant was mightily baffled by this, and said to the old man:

'Well, since you are so strong and so tough, such a hero of formidable strength, you should come with me to my cave. There are eight other Giants there, and each one of them is stronger then me, so they always make me go and run errands for them, as if I were the youngest. When we get to the cave, you will become the leader, and I will be next in line, so the rest of the Giants will listen to and respect us both. As the leader, you will have everything to your heart's content and more; just say what you want and the Giants will serve you as their elder.'

The old man agreed to go to the Giants' cave, and so they set forth. Along the way they came upon a cherry tree in season, heavy with ripe, red fruit, and as soon as the Giant saw it, he jumped up on it and beckoned the old man to join him. To this, the old man replied:

'I do not feel like climbing up; will you lower a branch for me so I can sit down and rest for a bit.'

The Giant did as the old man asked, bent and lowered the branch for him to sit on, but no sooner did the old man sit on it, then the branch bounced up and flung our old man over the cherry tree and into a bush, where there happened to be a hare, and in the fear and the commotion, the old man squashed the hare. Seeing this, the Giant laughed heartily and asked the old man what on earth happened to him? The old man said how from the top of the cherry tree he spotted a hare in the bush, and so he jumped from the tree to catch the hare for their dinner. Now the Giant marvelled even more at this display of virility, and he felt intimidated.

Thence they continued their journey and finally they reached the cave. There they found the other eight Giants and the old man greeted them all. The first Giant then recounted all the old man's heroics and the group agreed that he be their leader, and that they treat him as their elder. But when the old man began ordering and demanding not only what they had and could do but also what they didn't have and couldn't do, the Giants began to resent this and to plot a way to get rid of him. At first, they tested his strength; he had to prove he was as mighty a hero as their weakest brother had claimed and would have them believe. So they went out to a nearby meadow and held a boulder hurling contest. The Giants all picked a huge boulder each and tossed them off of their shoulders as if they were nothing but mere eggs. When it was the old man's turn, he began eyeing up the biggest of the boulders in the field, walked over to it, rolled up his sleeves and gazed over the mountaintops in the distance. The Giants then enquired what he was looking at, and the old man answered:

'I'm looking to see which hilltop to chuck this pebble over.'

When the Giants heard this, they looked at each other in bewilderment and asked the old man not to throw this boulder, as it was the best and the biggest one around, they weren't keen on parting with it. But the old man said:

'I will either have it my way, or no way at all.'

The Giants then agreed that he should not throw the boulder, and they will admit that he is the winner of this contest and the strongest one amongst them all.

Another time, they went to fetch water from a mountain spring. The Giants took a huge wineskin[2] each, and the old man took a shovel. As the Giants filled up their huge wineskins with water, the old man began digging around the spring. The Giants looked at each other in bewilderment and enquired what the old man was up to. The old man said:

'Why go fetch the water all the time when we can simply dig the spring out, carry it over to the cave and drink it all up in but a few days?'

When the Giants heard this, they were greatly alarmed at the thought of losing their spring and they demanded that the old man leave it be. But the old man said:

'I will either have it my way, or no way at all.'

The Giants then agreed that he should not dig the spring up, and they will admit that he is the winner of this contest and the strongest one amongst them all. The following day they all went to fetch firewood. The Giants pulled and uprooted a beech tree each, tossed it over their shoulders and turned to walk back to the cave, while the old man unravelled a pile of rope he brought along and began tying the trees one to another, as if he were about to uproot the whole forest. The Giants looked at each other in wonderment and asked the old man what he was up to. The old man replied:

'Why go fetch the firewood all the time when we can simply pull the whole forest out of the ground, carry it over to the cave and burn it all up in but a few days?'

When the Giants heard this, they were greatly alarmed at the thought of losing their forest and they tried to reason with the old man and dissuade him from pursuing this venture, but the old man said:

'I will either have it my way, or no way at all.'

The Giants then agreed that he should not uproot the forest, and they will admit that he is the winner of this contest, too and the strongest one amongst them all.

When the Giants saw that they couldn't overcome the old man, they began conspiring to find a way to be rid of him for good. Every night, the old man went to bed first, but couldn't sleep for a long while, and so he lay quietly under his blanket, waiting for the sleep to come. One night, whilst he lay awake under the covers, the Giants plotted to beat him up with spades and mallets in his sleep. One of them suggested they waited till the dead of night. So they all went to sleep for a while, intent on getting up later and putting their plan into action. But as soon as the Giants were all asleep, the old man got up and placed a pack saddle under his blanket, and he himself ran up and hid in the attic. When the Giants awoke in the dead of night, they grabbed the spades and the mallets and each of them walloped and larruped the old man's blanket several times, until the saddle all crumbled to dust, and the Giants rejoiced at the sound of the old man's bones being crushed under their blows. They agreed to throw the remains of the old man out in the morning, and went back to sleep. When the Giants were fast asleep, the old man descended from the attic, removed the crumbled remains of the saddle and lay back down under his blanket.

In the morning, he was the first one to rise and the Giants, as they woke one

18

after the other, rubbed their eyes and dropped their jaws in disbelief. At last, they enquired if the old man had slept well and if anything had disturbed his slumber? The old man said:

'I slept very well indeed, except for some bugs that kept biting me through the night.'

The Giants then saw that there was nothing they could do to this old man, so the following evening they conspired to throw boiling water over him, once again in the dead of night. But the old man overheard them plotting again and did the same as before, waited for them to fall asleep, placed another pack saddle under the blanket, waited for the Giants to finish pouring boiling water over his blanket and went back to his bed once they were all asleep. The next morning again he was the first to rise. The Giants could not believe their eyes when they saw him alive and well, and they enquired about his night's sleep. The old man replied to them:

'I slept very well indeed, except for some mild rain dripping down on me through the night, I think your roof may be in need of repair.'

Finally, the Giants decided to part ways with the old man and they informed him of this decision. The old man agreed to this, and he asked for a load of gold and riches, and for one of the Giants to carry the treasure and the old man on his back all the way to the watermill. The strongest of the Giants was assigned this task. The old man loaded the riches on the Giants back, climbed on his shoulders and they set forth, homeward bound. But by the time they reached the watermill, the Giant was out of breath, panting and gasping, heaving and wheezing; as they opened the door to the mill, he let out a big sigh of relief and the sheer might of his huff scattered the old man's children and sent them flying one up to the girder, the other one out the window, the third one up the chimney—not one of them stayed on the ground! When the Giant saw this, he dropped the old man and the load of gold in terror, and ran like greased lightning all the way back to the cave. When he reached his brethren, he recounted the miracle he had just witnessed:

'My', he said, 'as tough a hero as the old man may be, his children are even tougher. As soon as they saw me, they jumped up on the girder to bring the whole mill down on me, one of them went up the chimney and the other out the window to stop me from escaping, I barely managed to get out of there alive!'

Notes

1. A Giant is a mythical creature of supernatural size and strength. Similar to Cyclops in Greek and then Roman mythology, a Giant will often have only one eye, big bushy eyebrows and the ability to pull trees out by the roots, throw

boulders up into the heavens and bring houses down with a huff and a puff. Giants are born of Vilas, and their fathers are legendary folk heroes. They live in tribes or companies, and reside in mountain caves. Despite their physical strength, they are often depicted as dumb and gullible, so an old man or a child could overcome them with his wits ('brains over brawn'; to some extent also reminiscent of the biblical story of David and Goliath).

2. A wineskin is an animal skin sewn up and used as a container for holding and transporting liquids such as wine, water etc.

The Hovering Castle

Once upon a time there lived a Tzar who had three sons and one daughter, and this daughter he nourished and cherished and kept safe from all harm within the confines of his castle.

Time passed and the little girl turned into a young maiden. One evening, she asked her father to let her take a stroll outside the castle with her brothers, and the father consented to this request. No sooner did she step one foot outside, however, than a Zmaj[1] swooped down from the sky, snatched the maiden amidst her brothers and carried her up into the heavens and away. The brothers ran straight back to their father and imparted the news of their sister's demise, announcing how they wish to go and search for her. The father consented to this request and bestowed upon each of them a horse, and whatever else they needed for the journey, and so they set forth.

The brothers travelled far and wide and after some time they came upon a castle which was neither on the earth nor in the skies, but was hovering above the ground. As they reached the castle, they wondered if their sister might be up there, and began to forge a way to get inside. Upon long deliberation, they resolved that one of their horses be slain in order to sew its hide into a leather strap, fasten the strap to the head of an arrow and shoot the arrow vigorously with a bow into the walls of the castle, so that they could climb up the strap and over the walls. The two younger brothers then asked the eldest to slay his horse, but the eldest brother wished not to do this, and neither did the middle one, so the youngest brother slew his own horse, sewed its hide into a leather strap, fastened it to the head of an arrow and shot the arrow with a bow. When it came to scaling the walls, the eldest and the middle brother again eschewed the task and so the youngest one climbed the strap.

Having entered the castle, he went from door to door, from one room to the next, until he came upon a room where his sister sat with the Zmaj who was asleep, with his head resting in her lap while she groomed it. At the sight of her

25

brother she became greatly dismayed and besought him whisperingly to run for his life ere the Zmaj wakes. The brother refused to run and instead swung his mace at the Zmaj's head. Waking from his slumber, the Zmaj scratched the spot where the mace hit him and said:

' Something bit me right here.'

At this, the Tzar's youngest son swung his mace once more and the Zmaj said to the maiden:

'Again, something bit me here.'

As the young man swung his mace for the third time, his sister pointed at the place where the Zmaj's life force lay; no sooner did the mace hit the spot than the Zmaj dropped dead and the Tzar's daughter pushed him from her lap and ran to her brother, embraced and kissed him, then took him by the hand and led him through all the rooms in the castle.

First she took him to a room with a black horse at a trough, his tack all made of sterling silver. Then she took him through to another room, with a white horse at the trough, his tack all made of pure gold. And then she took him to a room where a dun horse was at the trough, with his tack all made of gems and precious stones. Next came a room where a maiden sat with a golden tambour hoop in her hands, embroidering with golden thread. Thence she took him to a room where another maiden sat, spinning the golden thread. At last she took him to a room where a third maiden sat, stringing pearls, and in front of her on a golden tray a golden hen and chicks pecked pearls.

Having seen all this, the young Tzarevich went back to the room where the dead Zmaj lay, dragged him out and threw him over the walls. When his brothers saw the dead Zmaj on the ground, they nearly fainted. Then the youngest lowered the sister first, then all of the three maidens with their handiwork, one after the other. As he lowered the maidens, he assigned one to each of his brothers, appointing the last one, the one with the hen and the chicks, to himself. His brothers envied his courage in finding and rescuing their sister, and so they cut the leather strap so he could not climb down. Then they found a young shepherd in the field, disguised him as their young brother and took him home to their father, threatening their sister and the maidens harshly, should they say a word of their misdeed to anyone.

After some time had passed, word of his brothers and the young shepherd marrying the maidens reached the young Tzarevich in the hovering castle. On the day of his eldest brother's wedding, he mounted the black horse and, just as the couple and the guests were leaving the church, swooped down amidst them and tapped his brother, the groom, on the back with his mace, so that the groom keeled over; then he flew back to the hovering castle.

On hearing the news of his middle brother's wedding day, the young Tzarevich

26

mounted the white horse and just as the wedding guests were coming out of the church, swooped down amidst them and tapped his middle brother, the groom, on the back with his mace in the same way so that the groom keeled over; then he flew back to the hovering castle.

At last, when he heard the news of the young shepherd marrying the maiden he had chosen for himself, he mounted the dun horse and flew to the wedding just as the guests were coming out of the church, and hit the groom over the head with his mace, killing him on the spot. The wedding guests then pounced on the Young Tzarevich to get him, but he did not run; instead he showed himself as the Tzar's real youngest son and told them how his envious brothers left him in the hovering castle where he had found their sister and slain the Zmaj. His sister and the maidens attested the truth of his account. Hearing this, the Tzar felt mightily angered at his two elder sons and immediately disowned and ousted them, giving his youngest son the maiden he had chosen in marriage and proclaiming him heir to the throne.

Notes

1. Zmaj [zmahy] /zmai/ is a mythical winged creature of extraordinary strength, similar to Aždaja (see The Young Tzarevich and the Aždaja, Note 5), with one or more heads. Whistling and howling resound through the land when he flies across the sky, his mouth and wings spitting fire. He has the ability to shape-shift into an eagle, snake, other animals or into a human. However, while Aždaja is simply an evil monster, Zmaj's attributes are very different. Often seen as a tribal protector and/ or an incarnation of the soul of a highly respected ancestor, Zmaj has a special place in the Serbian mythological pantheon. He can be either good or evil in relation to humans, depending on his personality and the specific set of circumstances (i.e. if angered, he will retaliate). Legend has it that Serbia gained a new Zmaj once a year, from a lake near a certain village; a fiery ball would rise into the sky and burst to pieces around midnight—one of these pieces would become a Zmaj, and the others would fly behind him in the night sky until his wings were fully developed and he had found a place to settle in. Zmajs were considered to be the protectors of the places (usually mountains) they settled in. A Zmaj was forever keen on marrying a beautiful maiden, and from this kind of marriage great heroes, Zmaj-children were born.

Zmaj is featured as a main character in a number of folk tales, legends, songs and poems, particularly following the Serbia's defeat by the Ottoman Empire in the Battle of Kosovo in 1389. From this point onwards, Zmajs became a symbol of the fight against the occupiers and represent great Serbian heroes, whilst Aždajas represent the Ottoman foes. According to folklore, Despot Stefan Lazarević was born from the union of the Zmaj of the Mountain Jastrebac and Princess Milica, and this marks the beginning of the Zmaj-hero genealogy.

Real Steel

Once upon a time there lived a Tzar who had three sons and three daughters. He lived a long life and when he reached a ripe old age, his time came to leave this world. On his deathbed, he summoned his sons and his daughters and asked his sons by testament to give their sisters' hands in marriage to the first suitors that came to the door. 'Give their hands in marriage', he said, 'lest you be damned'. And so he died.

After his death, when some time had passed, one night a banging was heard at the door: the whole palace shook; a howling, screeching, singing, flashing was heard, as if the palace were engulfed in flames. The palace inhabitants were overcome by fear and they shivered. Then, they heard a shout:

'Open up, Tzar's sons, open up the door!'

And the eldest Tzarevich said:

'Do not, DO NOT!'

But the youngest one declared:

'I shall open the door', then leapt and opened it.

No sooner did he open the door, than some sort of a creature entered—all they could see were the flames coming out of it, and it said:

'I came to ask the hand of your eldest sister in marriage, this very moment, to take her away, for I will not wait, nor will I ever come back to ask for her hand again; so answer me right now, will you give her hand to me or not?'

The eldest brother replied:

'I shall not give her hand to you. How could I do that, when I don't even know what you are nor where you have come from? You appear tonight out of nowhere, wishing to take her away immediately—I wouldn't even know where to go and visit my sister.'

And the middle one said:

'I shall not let you take my sister away tonight.'

But the youngest one spoke to them thus:

'I shall give her hand, even if you do not; don't you remember what our father requested on his deathbed?' Then he took his sister's hand and, proffering it to the creature, said:

'May she be happy and honourable with you.'

As their sister stepped over the threshold, all the palace attendants fell to the ground in fear. Thunder, lightning, howling, cracking was heard, the whole palace shook, but then it passed and a new day broke. At day break, they all went out to look for traces of the forceful creature around the Tzar's palace, but they could find none; not a trace to be seen anywhere.

The following night, around the same time, again the howling, screeching, singing, flashing was heard, and once more someone shouted at the door:

'Open up, Tzar's sons, open up the door!'

The Tzar's attendants were overcome by fear, and they opened the door to a terrifying force, which demanded:

'I came to ask your middle sister's hand in marriage; give the maiden to me.'

The eldest brother replied:

'I shall not give her hand to you.'

And the middle one said:

'I shall not let you take my sister.'

But the youngest one spoke thus:

'I shall give her hand; do you still not remember what our father requested on his deathbed?' Then he took his sister's hand and, proffering it to the creature, said:

'May she be happy and honourable with you.'

And the force led the maiden by the hand and left. The following day, at the crack of dawn, they went out again to look around the palace for traces of the force that took their sister, but not a trace was to be found, as if it had never happened.

On the third night once more the thunder and lightning and howling shook the palace from the ground, and a voice boomed outside:

'Open up!'

The Tzar's sons sprang to their feet and opened the door, and a mighty force entered and demanded:

'I came to ask for the hand of your youngest sister in marriage.'

The eldest and the middle brother replied:

'We shall not give our sister for the third night in a row, we truly must know at least for the youngest one who we are giving her to and where she is to go, so that we can come and visit our sister.'

But the youngest brother protested:

'I shall give her hand, even if you do not; have you forgotten what our father

31

hath said to us, on his deathbed, was it so long ago?'

Then he took his sister's hand and said:

'Here she is, take her, may she be happy and joyous with you!'

And the force took the maiden and disappeared that very moment, amidst a great clattering. The next morning, the brothers felt very worried about the fate of their sisters.

When some time had passed, the brothers sat down in counsel together:

'Dear God, what could have befallen our sisters, when we know not wither they were taken and by whom?'

At last, they decided with each other:

'We shall go and look for our sisters.'

Then they all prepared for the journey and set off. After having travelled for some time, they came upon a mountain and spent the whole day crossing it. As dusk fell, they decided to look for a place near water, to rest for the night. They came upon a lake, made shelter and made supper. When it was time to go to sleep, the eldest brother said:

'You go and sleep, and I will keep watch.'

So the two younger brothers fell asleep, and the eldest kept watch through the night. At some god-forsaken hour, the lake waters began to tremble and he jumped in fear, seeing something rise from the midst of the lake and move towards him: it was an horrid Aždaja with two big ears and it charged right at him. The Tzarevich reached for his sabre and cut the Aždaja's head off, then cut both of its ears off and put them in his pocket; he cast the body and the head back into the lake. At that moment the dawn broke, but the two younger brothers were still asleep, unaware of what their eldest brother had done. So he woke them, but did not say a thing to them. Thenceforth they continued their journey. At dusk, again they thought about finding a place to rest for the night, not least as they were beginning to feel frightened of the deep mountains they had trudged into. They came upon a small lake and decided to stay the night there. They lit a fire and made supper with whatever they had. This time, the middle brother said:

'You go and sleep, and I will keep watch tonight.'

So the other two went to sleep, and the middle brother kept watch. Suddenly, the lake began to tremble and shake and what was he to see! An Aždaja with two heads charging right at him and his brothers; but the Tzarevich sprang to his feet and cut both of its heads off with his sabre, then cut the ears off the heads and put them in his pocket, casting the rest back into the lake. His brothers were unaware of all this; they slept through the night. At daybreak, the middle brother called to them:

'Wake up my brothers and rise, it is time!'

And the other two jumped and at once began preparing to continue the

32

journey. Having travelled for some time, the brothers began to feel more and more affrighted, as they knew not what land they were in, nor whether they would be able to survive for much longer on the road thus, with their food supplies running out. So they prayed to God to bring them upon a village, a town or any kind of human settlement, as for three days in a row they had roamed the same wasteland with no end to it in sight. At long last, they came upon another lake, a big one, and agreed to stay the night there as, if they kept on travelling, they might not be able to find another lake to rest by. So they lit a big fire, had supper and prepared for sleep. This time, the youngest one said:

'You two go to sleep, and I will keep watch tonight.'

So the two older brothers went to sleep, and the youngest one kept watch, his eyes fixed on the lake. At some god-forsaken hour of the night, the whole lake began to tremble, a big splash came out of the water and over the fire, putting half of it out; the youngest brother reached for his sabre and stood right next to the fire. An Aždaja with no less than three heads then came out and charged at him and his sleeping brothers, but he took heart and, without waking his brothers, charged at the Aždaja thrice and cut all of its three heads off. Then he cut all the ears off and put them in his pocket, and cast the rest back into the lake. As he was busy doing this, the fire went out completely; not wishing to wake his brothers and having nothing to light the fire with, he walked off into the wasteland, looking for a flame of some kind, but could not see a thing in the darkness. At last he found a tree and climbed up; from the top of the tree, he saw a fire burning nearby, or so it seemed to him. He climbed down and went to fetch the embers for their fire. He walked for some while before he reached the place: it was a cave[1], and inside he saw a big fire and nine Giants sat around it, roasting two men on spits, one on each side of the fire, with a big cauldron full of slaughtered people resting right in the middle of it. Seeing this, the Tzar's youngest son became overcome with terror and wished to turn and go back, but it was too late. So he shouted:

'Good evening, my company! I have been looking for you for some time.'

The Giants greeted him back:

'God help thee, our comrade!'

Then the young Tzarevich said:

'I am your comrade forever, and I will give my life for you.'

'Well then,' the Giants replied, 'if you are truly our comrade, will you eat humans and join us in our feats?'

'I will', the young Tzarevich replied, 'whatever you do, I will do it, too.'

'In that case, come and join us! Take a seat', they offered.

So he joined them by the fire as they took the cauldron off and dished out the meat. The young Tzarevich helped himself, too; but surreptitiously he cast each bite over his shoulder, instead of in his mouth. When they had eaten all the roast, they said to him:

'Lets go hunting; tomorrow is another day and we shall need to eat again.'

All nine of the Giants set forth, and the young Tzarevich joined them as the tenth comrade.

'There is a Tzar's town nearby', they explained. 'We've been feeding ourselves off the townsfolk for many years.'

When they were close to the town, the Giants pulled two fir trees from the ground and took them along, and when they reached the town wall they rested one of the trees against it and called to the Tzarevich:

'Now, climb this fir tree and get on top of the wall; we shall then pass you the other one to hold by the top and heave over the other side of the wall, so that we can climb up and down the trees and into the town.'

He climbed to the top of the wall, then said to them:

'I know not what to do; I haven't been practising this and cannot throw the tree over; can one of you climb up here and show me what to do?'

One of the Giants then climbed up and heaved the fir tree over the wall, holding it by the top. As the Giant sat thus, the young Tzarevich reached for his sabre and cut his head off; the Giant's dead body dropped into the town. Then the Tzarevich said:

'Now come up, one at a time, so that I can get you over the wall.'

Unaware of what had happened to the first Giant, the others followed suit, one by one; the Tzarevich beheaded all nine of them, then carefully climbed down and into the town. Then he searched the town all over, but couldn't find a living soul. 'The Giants have cleared this town of people altogether!', he thought to himself. At long last, he found a tall tower, with the flame of a candle visible in one of the top rooms. He tried the door and it opened; then he went up the stairs to the top and into the lit room. And what was he to find there?—a room furnished with gold, silk and velvet, with no-one inside but a maiden lying on a bed, asleep. No sooner had he entered the room, than his eyes fixed on the maiden; she was so beautiful. At the same time, in the corner of his eye he spotted a snake[2], crawling up the bedside; as it reached the maiden it stretched out ready to bite her on the forehead. The young Tzarevich then ran with a knife in his hand and pierced the snake with it through the skull, then stuck it in the headboard, saying out loud:

'May no other hand but mine be able to take this knife out of this snake!'

He then rushed back out, climbed over the wall and down onto the other side. When he reached the Giants' cave, he grabbed some embers and went back to his brothers, who were still asleep. He then lit a fire; not long after dawn broke and he woke his brothers to continue their journey.

Later on that day, they stumbled upon a road leading to the very same town. A mighty Tzar lived there and each morning he walked the town shedding tears over his poor townsfolk who kept getting devoured by the Giants. The thought of his own daughter perishing in this way some day caused him a great deal of anguish. As he roamed the deserted streets of the town that morning, he noticed the fir trees pulled up by their roots, leaning against the town wall. When he reached the wall, he was astonished to encounter a miraculous sight: the nine Giants, the town's pests, lying on the ground with their heads cut off. This gave him great joy, and the surviving townsfolk gathered and began to pray for the health of their saviour, the slayer of the Giants. At that very moment, the Tzar's servants came with the news of a snake's failed attempt at biting his daughter. Hearing this, the Tzar rushed straight to his daughter's room in the tower, where what was he to find?—a snake nailed to the headboard of her bed with a knife! He then tried to take the knife out, but the knife would not budge in the slightest.

The Tzar then sent a decree to all four corners of his great Tzardom: that whomever had slain the Giants and nailed the snake to his daughter's headboard should come and claim his reward in the form of great riches and his daughter's hand. In no time, the word spread across his great Tzardom; by the Tzar's order, inns were to be opened by the sides of all the main roads, in order to enquire with each and every traveller whether they knew anything about the slayer of the Giants—any news of the hero was to be relayed to the Tzar instantly, and the hero himself was to be sent to the Tzar to claim his reward. As the Tzar decreed, so it was done: inns were opened by the side of the roads, and every single traveller stopped and enquired with.

In time, the three Tzar's sons who were looking for their sisters came upon one of the inns and decided to stay the night there. After dinner, the innkeeper joined them and began recounting his great deeds. Then he asked if any one of them had done anything heroic? The eldest of the three brothers said:

'The first night of this journey I have undertaken with my brothers, we slept by the side of a lake, in the middle of a mountainous wasteland. After we had supper, my brothers went to sleep and I kept watch. All of a sudden an Aždaja emerged from the lake and charged at us; I grabbed my sabre and cut its head off. If you don't believe me, here is my proof—ears from its head!' Then he got the ears out of his pocket and tossed them on the table.

Hearing this, the middle brother said:

'On our second night, I kept watch—and I killed a two-headed Aždaja. Here is my proof!' He then produced two pairs of ears and tossed them on the table.

The youngest brother kept silent through this conversation. So the innkeeper asked him:

'Young fellow, your brothers are great heroes—and what about you?'

'I achieved a little something, too', he said. 'On our third night on the road, we lodged by a lakeside again. My brothers went to sleep, and I kept watch. At some

35

godforsaken hour of the night, the lake trembled and shook and a three-headed Aždaja came out; it charged at us, but I grabbed my sabre and cut all three of its heads off; here are the ears as my proof, all six of them.'

His brothers and the innkeeper were astounded by this, but he continued:

'As the fire had gone out during this skirmish, I went to look for a flame. Thus roaming the mountainous wasteland, I came upon a cave with nine Giants inside –' and so he told them all as had befallen him and everything he accomplished that night; his listeners were in awe.

No sooner had the innkeeper finished hearing the young Tzarevich's story, than he ran and imparted the news to the Tzar; the Tzar rewarded him with money and instantly sent his aides to bring the three Tzar's sons to him. When they were brought, the Tzar asked the youngest one:

'Have you done all these great deeds in my town, slain the Giants and saved my daughter from her demise?'

'I have, my Tzar', he replied.

The Tzar then gave him the hand of his daughter in marriage, and made him next in line to the throne. He also offered to find good wives for the other two brothers and to give them palaces, but they told him they were already married. They then recounted the tale of their quest to find their sisters. Having heard this story, the Tzar kept only the youngest brother by his side and gave the others two great loads of gold for their journey back home to their own palace in their own Tzardom.

The youngest brother kept thinking about his sisters and wanting to continue searching for them but he felt sad to leave his wife behind; also, the Tzar disagreed with this quest. So the young Tzarevich quietly withered from worry about his sisters, day by day.

One day the Tzar went a-hunting, saying to his son-in-law:

'Stay in the palace while I am away; here are nine keys for you to keep—you can open three or four of the rooms with plenty of gold, silver and other riches inside, you can even open eight rooms; but you must not dare open the ninth one, for if you do, all hell will break loose.'

And so the Tzar departed and the young Tzarevich stayed in the palace. No sooner was the Tzar out of sight, however, than the young Tzarevich began opening the doors one after the other, finding all sorts of riches and treasure inside. As he reached the ninth room, he thought to himself: 'I went through so much in my life so far, why should I be frightened to enter a room!' And he opened the door. Inside, what was he to find?—a man chained by his knees and his elbows to four pillars with four iron chains going from the pillars to the man's neck; he was chained up so fast he could not move an inch. Before him there was a golden fountain, pouring water into a golden trough, and next to him a golden cup adorned with jewels. The man wanted to drink water, but could not reach it. The young Tzarevich was astounded to see this and drew back, but the man said to him:

'I beseech you by God, do come inside.'

The young Tzarevich stepped inside, and the man said:

'Do a good deed and give me a cup of water; rest assured you will gain an additional life from me for this.'

The young Tzarevich thought to himself: 'What could be better than to have two lives?' And so he filled the cup with water and passed it to the man; the man drank it all up.

'What is your name?' The young Tzarevich asked.

'Real Steel³', the man replied.

The young Tzarevich then turned to leave, but the man beseeched him again:

'Please give me another cup of water, and I will bestow another life upon you.'

The young Tzarevich thought to himself: 'It is a miracle, to gain two more lives on top of the one I already have!' And so he filled another cup of water and gave it to the man, and the man drank it all up. As the young Tzarevich turned to go again, the man called to him:

'O young hero, come hither once more; since you already did two good deeds you could do a third one, and I will bestow a third life upon you. Take this cup and fill it up with water, then pour it over my head; for this, I will give you a third life to live.'

Hearing this, the young Tzarevich turned back, filled the cup with water and poured it over the man's head. As he poured the water, the rings around his neck burst open, as did all the chains that held Real Steel prisoner, and he leaped and spread his wings, and flew out the door. On his way from the palace, he snatched the Tzar's daughter, the wife of his saviour, and disappeared from sight. Now the real trouble began: the young Tzarevich was terrified of what the Tzar's reaction would be to this. That very moment, the Tzar returned from his hunting expedition and his son-in-law had no other choice but to impart everything as had happened. The Tzar was devastated to hear this, and asked the young Tzarevich:

'Why on Earth did you do this? Didn't I tell you not to open the ninth room?'

His son-in-law replied:

'Please do not be angry with me; I shall go and search for Real Steel and get my wife back.'

The Tzar then tried to dissuade him from this venture:

'Do not go, under any circumstances! You don't know who Real Steel is; I lost many a soldier and a whole lot of gold before I managed to catch and enslave him. Stay here with me and fear not: I still love you as my son and I shall find you another maiden to marry.'

But the young Tzarevich would not heed this and insisted on going in search of his wife and Real Steel; so he took some money, jumped on his horse and set out on his journey. He travelled for some time and at long last came upon a town. He looked around the town for a while, before he heard a maiden call out to him from a tower:

'Hey, young Tzarevich, get off your horse and come into my courtyard.'

He dismounted his horse and walked in to meet the maiden, and at once he recognised her: it was his eldest sister. They embraced and kissed joyfully, then she took him inside. When they got inside, the young Tzarevich asked his sister about her mysterious husband.

'My husband is a Zmaj, and he is the Tzar of them all', she said. 'But I must hide you, as he has vowed to kill his brothers-in-law at first sight. I shall test the waters first; if it seems like he won't kill you, I will tell him about you being here.'

And so she hid her brother and his horse. In the evening, at dinner time, the Zmaj came home. As he entered, the palace all glistened and shone. No sooner had he come in, than he called to his wife:

'My wife, I can smell a man in here; tell me who it is!'

'No-one', she replied.

'That cannot be', he said.

'Let me ask you something', his wife then said. 'If my brothers were to come and visit, would you harm them in any way?'

'I would, the eldest and the middle one—I would slaughter then roast them; I wouldn't do a thing to the youngest one, though', he replied.

'Well, my youngest brother, your brother-in-law, is here', she then said.

Hearing this, the Zmaj Tzar exclaimed:

'Get him over here!'

When the young Tzarevich was brought to the Zmaj Tzar, they embraced and kissed joyfully.

'Welcome, my brother-in-law!'

'Thank you, my Tzar!'

They talked for a while and the young Tzarevich recounted everything as had happened to him. Then the Zmaj Tzar said:

'What are you trying to do? The day before yesterday, Real Steel passed by here, carrying your wife. I met him with seven thousand soldiers, each one of them a Zmaj, and we could not overcome him. Drop this futile search; I'll give you some money, go back home.'

But the young Tzarevich would not yield. The following day, as he was about to set off and continue his search, the Zmaj Tzar, seeing that he could not dissuade him from this venture, pulled a feather from his wings and, proffering it to the

38

young Tzarevich, said:

'Listen to me carefully: here's a feather of mine; when you have found Real Steel and are in great need of help, set this feather on fire and I shall come with my entire army to your rescue.'

The young Tzarevich took the feather and left. He travelled for some time before he came upon another town. As he looked around the town, again he heard a maiden call to him from a tower:

'Hey, young Tzarevich, get off your horse and step inside my courtyard!'

As he entered the courtyard with his horse, he found that the maiden was his middle sister; they embraced and kissed joyfully. Then she took the horse to the stable and her brother up to the top of the tower, where he recounted all as has happened to him since last they saw each other. Then he asked her about her mysterious husband, and she said:

'My husband is a Falcon, the Tzar of all Falcons and he shall be here this evening; I must hide you before he returns, as he has threatened to kill my brothers many times.'

And so she hid her brother. Not long after, the mighty Falcon Tzar returned; the tower shook as he entered. His dinner was laid out at once, but he did not look at it and said to his wife:

'There is a man in here.'

'No, there isn't!' his wife replied.

Then she spoke to him for some while, before asking:

'If my brothers were to come and visit, would you do them any harm?'

'I would, to the eldest and the middle one, do a lot of harm', he replied. 'But I wouldn't harm the youngest one in the slightest.'

Then she told him about her youngest brother's visit. Hearing this, the Falcon Tzar at once sent for the young Tzarevich; they embraced and kissed joyfully.

'Welcome, my brother-in-law!' The Falcon Tzar greeted him.

'Thank you, my Tzar!' he replied.

Then they sat down to eat. After dinner, the Falcon Tzar enquired about his brother-in-law's journey, and the young Tzarevich told him all about Real Steel and how he was in search of him, intending to rescue his wife. But the Falcon Tzar advised him thus:

'Do not pursue this futile search any longer', he said. 'The very same day he snatched your wife, he passed by here and I met him with a five thousand-strong army of Falcons; we battled fiercely and plenty of blood was shed, but we could not overcome him; how are you intending to beat him alone?! My advice to you is to go back home; here is some money for the road, take as much as you want.'

But the young Tzarevich replied:

'I thank you, my Tzar, for your advice; but I shall not give up my search for Real

Steel.' While saying this out loud, quietly he thought to himself: 'Why would I give up the search, when I have been bestowed three more lives!'

Seeing that it was not possible to dissuade his brother-in-law from his intended feat, the Falcon Tzar pulled a feather from his wings and handed it over to him:

'Here', he said, 'here is a feather from my wings. When you are in great need, set this feather on fire and I shall come with my entire army to your rescue.'

The young Tzarevich took the feather and set off. Having travelled for some time, he came upon a third town. No sooner did he enter the town, than a maiden called to him from a tower:

'Get off your horse and come inside!'

The young Tzarevich dismounted his horse and walked into the yard; there he found the maiden to be his youngest sister; they embraced and kissed joyfully. She then took his horse to the stable and her brother to the top of the tower, where he asked her about her mysterious husband.

'My husband is an Eagle, the Tzar of all Eagles', she said.

When her husband returned in the evening, he said to his wife:

'There is a man in here, tell me who it is!'

'There's no-one here', she replied and they sat to dinner. Then she asked:

'If my brothers were to come and visit, what would you do?'

And her husband replied:

'I would kill the eldest and the middle one, but wouldn't do any harm to the youngest one. Instead, I would come to his aid any time.'

Then his wife revealed the truth:

'My youngest brother is here, he came to visit us.'

Hearing this, the Eagle Tzar at once sent for the young Tzarevich, and embraced and kissed him joyfully.

'Welcome, my brother-in-law!'

'Thank you, my Tzar!'

Then they sat down to eat. After dinner they talked about many things, and at long last the young Tzarevich told him about his quest for Real Steel. The Eagle Tzar advised him thus:

'Give up, my brother-in-law, this futile search, do not pursue it any longer. Stay here with me, you won't be lacking a thing here.'

But his brother-in-law would not listen, and the very next day set to continue his quest. Seeing that there was no way of reasoning with him, the Eagle Tzar pulled a feather from his wings and, proffering it to the young Tzarevich, said:

'Here, take this feather of mine. When you are in dire need, set this feather on fire and I shall come to your aid at once, with my entire army of Eagles.'

The young Tzarevich took the feather and set off.

He travelled from village to village, from town to town until, at long last, he came upon a cave and found his wife inside. She was greatly astonished to see him, and said:

'My dear husband, what on Earth are you doing here?'

And he recounted everything as had befallen him, then said:

'My wife, lets go, now!'

But she replied:

'Where are we to go? Real Steel will find us instantly and kill you first, then take me back!'

The young Tzarevich knew he had three more lives to live, so he reassured his wife and convinced her to run away with him, and they did. No sooner did they start running, than Real Steel got wind of it and chased them, caught up with them and shouted:

'Young Tzarevich, are you stealing my wife?' Then he grabbed hold of the wife and said to the young Tzarevich:

'I will let you go this time, as I remember I gave you three lives; but do not dare come back for her again, for you shall perish for sure next time!'

With this, Real Steel carried off his wife and the young Tzarevich stood alone and at a loss. At last, he decided to go back for his wife, waited outside the cave until Real Steel was gone and then got his wife to escape with him once more. Again, Real Steel knew of their flight straight away, ran after them, caught up with the young Tzarevich and asked:

'Would you prefer to be shot by arrows or cut by a sabre?'

The young Tzarevich pleaded for his life, and Real Steel said:

'I'll let you go one more time and let you use your second life but I'm telling you: do not dare come back for your wife again for I will not give you another life, I shall kill you on the spot next time!'

With this, Real Steel carried off the wife, and young Tzarevich remained on his own, still thinking about saving her. At last, he said to himself: 'Why should I be afraid of Real Steel, when I have two more lives left, one of his and one of my own?' So he decided to go back for his wife, when Real Steel was out again. He went to get her; once more, she protested it would be in vain. Eventually, however, he persuaded her and they started running again. Real Steel was after them at once and, when he caught up with them, proclaimed:

'There, your luck has run out, I shall not forgive you this time!'

The young Tzarevich felt overcome by fear and pleaded for his life, but Real Steel said:

'You remember I gave you three lives? I shall let you use the third one now, and that's my final boon. Go home now, lest you lose your own one life.'

Seeing that he could not overcome Real Steel, the young Tzarevich turned to go back home, but could not get the thought of rescuing his wife out of his mind.

Suddenly, he remembered the words of his brothers-in-law, and the feathers that they each had given him. Then he said to himself, resolutely: 'I shall go back and for the fourth time attempt to get my wife back, and if I end up in dire straits, I shall set these feathers on fire and my brothers-in-law will come to my rescue.' At once he returned to the cave and, seeing Real Steel walking off into the distance, he called to his wife. She was confounded to see him once more.

'Have you really no desire to live any longer, since you came back for me again?!'

He then told her about his brothers-in-law and the feathers they had each given him, promising to come to his aid when he needed them.

'That's why I have come back for you once more, lets go!'

So they ran, but Real Steel was after them in the blink of an eye and called to him:

'Stop, young Tzarevich, you're not going anywhere!'

Seeing Real Steel right behind them, the young Tzarevich took the three feathers out and lit a match, then began setting the feathers on fire. But by the time he set all three feathers on fire, Real Steel had caught up with them and cut the young Tzarevich in half with his sword. At that very moment, a miracle! The Zmaj Tzar, the Falcon Tzar, the Eagle Tzar and all their armies arrived, charging at Real Steel in full force; plenty of blood was shed, yet Real Steel managed to snatch the wife again and disappeared. The three Tzars then thought to give life back to their brother-in-law, and asked the three fastest ones in the Zmaj army which one could fetch water from the river Jordan[4] in the shortest time.

The first one said:

'I can do it in half an hour.'

The second one said:

'I can do it in quarter of an hour.'

The third one said:

'I can do it in nine seconds.'

So the Tzars sent the third one and he came back in nine seconds indeed. The Tzars then took the water and poured it over the cut: the young Tzarevich was put together once more and he sprang to his feet. Then his brothers-in-law advised him thus:

'Now go home, since you have been saved from certain death.'

The young Tzarevich replied how he was intending to go and try his luck one more time and rescue his wife, one way or another. His brothers-in-law tried to dissuade him:

'Do not pursue this any longer; you shall truly lose your life this time, since you have none left now bar your own.'

But he would not be swayed. So the Tzars gave him this counsel:

'Since you will not give up, then go but do not take your wife; tell her instead to ask Real Steel where his great strength lies, then come and tell us where it is and we will help you overcome him.'

The young Tzarevich went and taught his wife how to question Real Steel, then went back to his brothers-in-law. When Real Steel had returned to the cave, the wife began to enquire:

'Pray tell me, where does your great strength lie?'

And Real Steel replied:

'My dear wife, my strength lies in my sword.'

She then fell to her knees in prayer by the sword. Seeing this, Real Steel burst out laughing and said:

'Silly woman, my strength does not lie in my sword, but in my arrow.'

Then she fell to her knees in prayer by the arrow and Real Steel said:

'O my dear wife, someone clearly taught you well to trick me into telling you where my strength lies! If your husband were alive, I would have sworn it was him.'

She reassured him and swore how no-one had taught her to trick him, for there was no-one who could.

A few days later, her husband returned and she told him how she could not find out anything from Real Steel; her husband told her to keep trying. So when Real Steel came back home, she began enquiring after his strength again. Real Steel replied:

'Since you have such great respect for my strength, I shall tell you the truth:

On a far, far away mountain, there is a fox; and in that fox, there is a heart; and in that heart, there is a bird, and in that bird—that's where my strength lies. The thing is, the fox cannot be caught so easily; it can shape-shift into many things.'

The following day, when Real Steel was gone, the young Tzarevich returned once more to hear if his wife had managed to get the truth about Real Steel's strength. She told him all as she heard from Real Steel; he went straight to his brothers-in-law, who were eagerly awaiting to hear from him and were ready to go after Real Steel's strength. So all four of them ventured to the far away mountain and when they arrived, they sent the Eagles to hunt for the fox. The fox ran and hid in a lake, then shape-shifted into a wild goose. The Falcons then chased the goose out of the lake and the goose flew into the sky, where it was chased by an army of Zmajs. It then quickly shape-shifted back into a fox and began running across the mountain, but the Eagles and the rest of the armies ambushed her there and caught her. Then at the Tzars' command the fox was cut open and its heart taken out; a big fire was lit, too. They cut the heart open then, took the bird out and threw it on the fire. As the bird burnt to death, so Real Steel was no more. Then the young Tzarevich finally got his wife and took her back home.[5]

43

Notes

1. In Slavic and Serbian folklore, caves belong to the category of mythical places (see also: The Young Tzarevich and the Aždaja, Note 4, Watermill). Often found in the mountainous areas, caves provide a natural shelter. Their physical qualities have always captured people's imagination: the varying shapes of rock, the mysterious ways in which the sound travels and the underground streams lend themselves perfectly to interpretation as places teeming with spirits and mythical creatures. They are the home of Giants, hiding places of Vilas, but also entry points for the netherworld: Slavs believed that this realm belonged to the dead, but that it was possible for the living to enter it, too—not so easy to return from, though. During the Ottoman rule, caves were also the hiding places for hajduks—the outlaws, bandits and freedom fighters who rose against the foreign occupiers, but also frequently robbed the rich (kinds of Balkan Robin Hood characters).

2. According to Serbian folklore, a snake is a demonic animal, created by the Devil himself.

3. Real Steel is a mythical creature of extraordinary strength, man made of steel.

4. The river Jordan flows through the Jordan Rift Valley into the Dead Sea. It is a key water resource for the area (and, as such, a source of conflict between Israel, Jordan, Lebanon, Syria and the Palestinians). It has a further significance in Christian tradition as the scene of the baptism of Jesus by John the Baptist, among many other mentions in the Bible and the New Testament. Here, it is a perfect example of Christianity's accommodation of pagan beliefs: while the notion of 'live water' existed in Slav mythology from the earliest days (see: The Golden-fleeced Ram, Note 5, Live water), i.e. special kind of water that has magical healing powers, including resurrection and reattachment of severed body parts, by associating it with the holy water from the most holy of rivers in the Christian tradition, the Christian church incorporates the belief, assimilating it to become part of its own doctrine.

5. Many of the motifs from this tale can be found in the Russian tale *Maria Morevna*: the mysterious, supernatural suitors; the forbidden room; the character of Real Steel. Some elements of the plot are very similar, too—but there are also many differences in detail, reflecting the differences in folklore between the two nations.

The Golden Apple Tree and the Nine Peahens

Once upon a time there lived a Tzar who had three sons. In the Tzar's garden there grew a golden apple tree, and this tree would blossom and bear fruit over night; but before the night was over, someone would pick all the fruit and no-one knew who was to blame for this. One day the Tzar said to his sons:

'I would like to know who is taking the fruit from our apple tree.'

The eldest son replied:

'I will keep watch tonight and find out who is picking the apples.'

In the evening, the son went and lay down under the tree to keep watch, but as the apples ripened he fell asleep and when he woke in the morning, the fruit was all gone. So he went to his father and told him what had happened. The second son then offered to keep watch by the tree, but he had no better luck: he also fell asleep in the middle of the night, and when he woke in the morning not a single fruit was left on the tree. Then it was the youngest son's turn to keep watch. He prepared well and brought his bed under the tree, then lay down to sleep. He woke up just before midnight, in time to see the apples ripening—the whole palace was lit up by their shimmering. At that very moment, nine peahens flew over, eight of them alighting on the tree and the ninth one on his bed. As she touched down, she turned into a beautiful maiden, such as could not be found in the whole Tzardom. They caressed each other till after midnight; the maiden then rose and thanking him for the apples, prepared to depart. The young Tzarevich beseeched her to leave him one apple at least and she gave him two: one for him and one for his father. Then she turned into a peahen again and flew away with the other eight. When he woke in the morning he took the two apples to his father. The Tzar was delighted to see this and he praised his youngest son. In the evening again the youngest son made his bed under the tree and lay in it to keep watch; everything happened as the night before and in the morning he took two apples back to his father once more. But after he succeeded in guarding the apple tree thus for several nights in a row, his brothers began to grow envious of him, as he could accomplish so well what they could not do. So they went to an old woman, who promised to find out for them how he managed to save two apples from the tree each night. In the evening, she sneaked up and hid under their brother's bed below the tree. Not long after, the Tzar's youngest son arrived and lay on his bed as usual. Just before midnight, the nine peahens appeared; eight of them alighting on the apple tree and the ninth one on the young man's bed, turning into a beautiful maiden as soon as she touched down. Carefully, by stealth, the old woman grasped one of the maiden's plaits as it hung by the side of the bed and cut it off; instantly the maiden leaped from the bed and turned back into a peahen, then flew away with the other eight and disappeared in the distance. The Tzar's youngest son leaped from the bed, too, and cried:

'What was that?!' Then he looked under the bed and, seeing the old woman dragged her out; the next morning he had her drawn and quartered[1]. The peahens, however, never came back to the apple tree and the Tzar's youngest son wept and mourned his loss. At long last, he decided to go and search the world for his peahen, resolving never to come back unless he found her. Hearing this, his father the Tzar implored him not to go, and tried to dissuade him from this venture by promising to find him another maiden to marry, any one he desired in the whole Tzardom. But all the Tzar's pleas were in vain; the young man could not be swayed. He took one servant along on this quest and they set off into the great wide world.

Having travelled far and wide, they came upon a lake with a grand palace next to it. In the palace they found an old Tzaritza[2] and her only daughter. The Tzar's youngest son asked:

'Do you happen to know, grandma Tzaritza, anything about the nine golden peahens?'

And the old Tzaritza replied:

'O my dear child, I know of them, indeed—they come to bathe in this very lake every day at noon. But you should forget about the peahens; look at my lovely daughter and all these riches—you could inherit all this, should you marry her instead.'

But the young man would not even listen to her, let alone consider her offer; he was burning with desire to see the peahens. So the next morning, at the crack of dawn, he went straight to the lake to wait for them. Meanwhile the old Tzaritza bribed his servant and gave him a pair of bellows, instructing him thus:

'When you get to the lake, take these bellows and gently blow down your master's neck; he will then fall asleep in an instant and will not be able to talk to the peahens.'

The wretched servant did as he was told; when he joined his master at the lakeside, he waited for a good opportunity then blew the bellows down his neck, and his master fell asleep at once. No sooner did he fall asleep, than the nine peahens appeared. As they arrived, eight of them alighted on the lake and the ninth one on his horse's back beside him; she caressed him and tried to wake him:

'Awake, my darling! Awake, my soul! Arise, my heart!' But he did not stir, as if he were dead.

Having finished bathing in the lake, all the nine peahens flew away. At this very moment, the Tzar's youngest son woke up and asked his servant:

'What of the peahens? Have they been here yet?'

And the servant told him how they came and how eight of them alighted on the lake and the ninth one on his horse's back beside him, and how she caressed him and tried to wake him. Hearing this, the poor Tzar's son despaired so much he wished he could die. The very next day, again they went to the lake. The Tzar's son paced up and down on horseback by the lakeside, so as not to fall asleep again, but the wicked servant spied a good opportunity once more and blew the bellows down his neck; he fell asleep instantly. No sooner did he fall asleep, than the nine peahens alighted; eight of them on the lake and the ninth one on his horse's back beside him. Again she caressed him and tried to wake him:

'Awake, my darling! Awake, my soul! Arise, my heart!' Alas, all this to no avail: it was as if he were dead.

Then she said to the servant:

'Tell your master: tomorrow still he can meet us here; after that we shall never come back.'

And they all flew away. The moment they were gone, the Tzar's son woke up and asked his servant:

'Have they been here yet?'

And his servant replied:

'They have, and they left you a message: you can still meet them here tomorrow; after that, they shall never return to this place.'

The Tzar's son was so devastated to hear this, he pulled his own hair out in despair.

So for the third day in a row, they went to the lake to meet the peahens. In order to prevent himself from falling asleep again, the Tzar's son galloped on his horse by the lake. Nonetheless, the servant still managed to find an opportune moment and blew the bellows down his neck; at once, he fell asleep, seconds before the peahens appeared. As they arrived, eight of them alighted on the lake and the ninth one on his horse beside him; caressing him gently, she tried to wake him:

'Awake, my darling! Awake, my soul! Arise, my heart!' Alas, to no avail: he slept on as if he were dead. The peahen then said to the servant:

'Tell your master he will see me next after he's seen a pig fly.' With that, they all took off. No sooner were they out of sight than the Tzar's son woke up and asked the servant:

'Have they been here?'

'They have,' the servant replied. 'The one who alighted on your horse left you a message—to go and find a flying pig, and then you shall find her, too.'

Hearing this, the Tzar's son drew his sword and cut the servant's head off. After that he roamed the world alone for some while until, at long last, he came upon a mountain. There he found a hermit and asked him if he knew anything about the nine golden peahens.

The hermit replied:

'My dear son, you are very fortunate and led by God on your path. They are half a day's walk from here. Just go straight until you reach a big gate; once you've passed through the gate keep right and you will come upon their city and inside it, their palace.'

The Tzar's son stayed the night in the hermit's cave and in the morning he thanked his host and continued his journey. Some while later he came upon the gate, passed through it and turned right; around midday, his heart leapt at the sight of a white city shining bright in the distance. He found his way to the peahens' palace; he was stopped and questioned by the guards at the door. He told them who he was and where he had come from; when they imparted this to his peahen, the Tzaritza, she ran like greased lightning, in her maiden shape, to welcome him in. Great joy ensued; a few days later they got married and he settled in her palace.

One day, after some time had passed, the Tzaritza went out for a stroll. On her way out, she handed keys to twelve cellars to her husband, saying to him:

'You can enter any one of the cellars, except for the twelfth one; you mustn't go there, under any circumstances!' And with that, she left.

The Tzar's son wondered: 'What could the twelfth cellar hold?' Then he began opening them one after the other. When he reached the twelfth one, at first he was not going to open it, but eventually curiosity got the better of him, he could no longer resist the temptation to take a peek and see what was inside; so he opened the door. There he found a big wooden barrel bound fast with three iron hoops and a voice came out of the barrel:

'For the love of God, my brother, give me a glass of water, I am dying of thirst!'

The Tzar's son filled a glass with water then poured it into the barrel through a hole on the top; no sooner did he do this, than one of the hoops burst open. Again, he heard the voice:

'For the love of God, my brother, give me another glass of water, I am dying of thirst!'

So the Tzar's son poured another glass of water into the barrel, and another one of the hoops burst open. For a third time the voice came out:

'For the love of God, my brother, give me one more glass, I am dying of thirst!'

The Tzar's son poured a third glass of water in and the third hoop burst open; the barrel then fell to pieces and a Zmaj flew out and away, seizing the strolling Tzaritza on his way. Her maids saw this and came with the news to the Tzar's son; he was devastated to hear what had happened to her. Not knowing what else to do, the Tzar's son once more set off in search of his peahen.

Having roamed the world for some while thus, he came upon a lake and, next to it, a little puddle of water with a fish flapping about in it. Seeing the Tzar's son, the little fish begged:

'My brother-with-God³, I beseech you, throw me back into the lake. Some day I will be of use to you; just take one of my scales and, when you need my help, rub it gently between your palms.'

The Tzars' son took the fish out of the puddle, pulled one of its scales off and wrapped it in a handkerchief, then threw the fish back into the lake.

Some while later, he came upon a fox caught in an iron trap. Seeing him, the fox implored:

'My brother-with-God, release me from these irons! Some day I shall be of good use to you; just take one of my hairs and, when you need me most, rub it gently between your palms.'

The Tzar's son pulled a hair from the fox, then set if free.

Further on, as he travelled across a mountain, he came upon a wolf caught in an iron trap. Seeing him, the wolf too implored:

'My brother-with-God, please set me free. I shall come to your aid some day; just take one of my hairs and, when you are in need, rub it gently between your palms.'

The Tzar's son pulled one of the wolf's hairs out and set him free.

The Tzar's son then continued his journey and, some while later, he met a man on the road.

'Tell me, my brother, would you happen to know the whereabouts of the Zmaj Tzar's palace?' he asked.

The man gave him good directions to the palace, as well as the length of time it should take him to reach it. The Tzar's son thanked him and went on; it was a long while before he finally reached the city of the Zmaj Tzar. He found his peahen in the Zmaj's palace, and they rejoiced greatly at seeing each other. They pondered what to do next, and decided to run away; with great haste they mounted their horses and galloped away. No sooner were they out of sight, however, than the Zmaj Tzar returned to the palace on his horse. When he entered the palace he found the Tzaritza gone and said to the horse:

'What are we to do now? Sit down and have our dinner, or go and chase after them?'

And the horse replied:

'Sit down and have your dinner and worry not: we shall yet catch up with them.'

Having eaten his dinner, the Zmaj sat on his horse and gave chase; in no time he caught up with them and snatched the Tzaritza away from the Tzar's son, saying to him:

'I'll let you go this time, since you gave me water before in the cellar; but take care not to come back, lest you wish to lose your life.'

The Tzar's son, in his misery, rode his horse on for a short distance but, unable to resist his heart's yearning, he turned back and the next day re-entered the palace. There he found his Tzaritza alone, in tears. They conferred for some time again, wondering what to do next, until the Tzar's son said:

'When the Zmaj comes back, ask him where he obtained that horse of his—I shall then look for another one of the kind, and perhaps we shall be able to escape the Zmaj thus.' With this, he left.

When the Zmaj Tzar returned, the peahen Tzaritza began to fawn on him and to flatter him and, at length, asked:

'Your horse is so fast! Where on earth did you get him?'

And the Zmaj replied:

'I got him from a very special place, where not everyone can get a horse from. On a certain mountain, there lives an old witch-woman[4] who has twelve beautiful horses in her stables, each one better than the last. In the far corner of the stable, there is a scraggly looking horse—a leper, one might think, but in truth—he is the best horse ever and he is the brother of my own horse. One who gets this horse will be able to fly into the sky on it. However, one must serve the old woman for three days before he may obtain this horse: the old woman has a mare and a foal, and one must look after them for three nights in a row before he can claim his prize; if he succeeds in keeping watch over them, he can choose any horse from her stable in reward. But if he fails to keep the mare and the foal safe, he shall lose his head.'

The following day, when the Zmaj left the palace, the Tzar's son returned and the Tzaritza recounted everything she had heard from the Zmaj to him. So the Tzar's son went to the said mountain and found the old witch-woman.

'God help thee, grandma!' he greeted her.

'God help thee, my child,' she replied. 'What brings you here?'

'I'd like to serve you,' the Tzar's son said.

To this, the old woman retorted:

'All right, my son. If you succeed in keeping my mare safe for three days in a row, you can ask for any horse from my stable in return; and if you do not manage to keep her safe, you shall lose your head.'

Then she took him through to her yard, wherein stood stake after stake, each with a human head planted on top, bar one—and this empty stake cried incessantly:

'Give me a head, grandma! Give me a head!'

Having shown him through her yard, the witch said:

'See, all these heads belonged to people who came to serve me and to look after my mare; they couldn't look after the mare well so they lost their heads!'

But the Tzar's son was not put off by this in the slightest and stayed to serve the witch. In the evening, he mounted the mare and rode her into a field; the foal followed. He sat upon the mare keeping watch; around midnight, however, he dozed off and when he woke up he found himself sitting upon a log, holding tightly onto the reins in his hands. He was greatly alarmed at this, and instantly leapt to his feet and went in search of the mare. He came upon a lake and at the first sight of it, remembered the little fish he saved from the puddle; he took the fish scale out from his handkerchief and rubbed it gently between his palms; at that very moment the little fish called out:

'What is happening, my brother-with-God?'

'The old woman's mare escaped and I can't find her,' he replied.

And the little fish said:

'She's down here with us, she turned into a fish and so has her foal; just hit the water with the reins and say these words: 'Easy, old woman's mare!''

So the Tzar's son did as he was told and instantly the mare regained her true shape, as did her foal; they came out of the lake and he mounted her and rode her back to the old woman's house, with the foal in tow. When he arrived, the witch gave him food to eat and took the mare to the stable, where she beat her with a poker and yelled:

'You should have gone amidst the fish in the lake!'

'I did,' the mare replied, 'but the fishes are his friends and they informed on me.'

And the witch said:

'Well then, go to the foxes next!'

The following evening, the Tzar's son mounted the mare again and rode her into the field; the foal galloped by her side. Once again, around midnight, he nodded off astride the mare and when he woke a short while later, he found himself atop a log, with the reins in his hands. Startled, he jumped to go and search for her at once. Then he remembered the old woman's words to the mare he had overheard the night before; he took his handkerchief out and gently rubbed the fox hair—the fox appeared before him instantly.

'What ails you, my brother-with-God?' she asked.

And the Tzar's son replied:

'The old woman's mare has run away, and I don't know where she is.'

'She's here, among us,' the fox replied. 'She turned into a fox and her foal into a cub; hit the ground with the reins and say: 'Easy, old woman's mare!''

So he hit the ground with the reins and he called the mare; she turned up before him with her foal, both in their true shape. He mounted her and rode back to the old woman's house, with the foal in tow. When he arrived, the old woman gave him dinner and took the mare to the stable; beating her with a poker, she cried:

'Why didn't you go among the foxes, you cursed mare!?'

'I did,' the mare replied. 'But the foxes too are his friends and they informed on me.'

'Well then, you should go among the wolves next!' the old woman said.

For the third night in a row, the Tzar's son mounted the mare and led the foal to the field. And for the third night in a row, he fell asleep atop the mare. When he woke, he found himself sitting upon a log, holding the reins in his hands. He ran to go and look for them, then remembered the old woman's words to the mare from the night before; he took the wolf's hair from his handkerchief and rubbed it gently between his palms. In an instant, the wolf appeared before him.

'What is troubling you, my brother-with-God?'

'The old woman's mare escaped again, I don't know where to find her.'

And the wolf replied:

'She's here, among us; she turned into a wolf and her foal into a wolf cub. Hit the ground with the reins and shout: 'Easy, old woman's mare!''

So he did; the mare and foal appeared before him at once, and he rode on her back to the old woman's house, the foal galloping along. Upon arrival at the old woman's house, he was given dinner; the old woman took the mare to the stable and, brandishing her poker, said:

'You should have gone to the wolves, wretched mare!'

'And I did,' the mare replied. 'The wolves are also his friends, and they informed on me.'

As the old woman came out of the stable, the Tzar's son went up to her and said:

'So, grandma, I have served you in earnest and now I wish to claim my reward.'

And the old woman replied:

'My son, as we agreed, so it shall be. Here, choose any among these twelve horses.'

'Why should I be too picky,' the Tzar's son said. 'I am not fit for the beautiful ones; I want the scraggly one in the corner.'

The old woman tried to dissuade him from this choice:

'Why choose the scraggly one, when you can have any of the fine ones!'

But the Tzar's son held his ground:

'You said I could have whichever one I chose; I want the scraggly one.'

Having no way out of this arrangement, the old woman eventually succumbed to his request and gave him the horse he chose. He took leave of the old woman, and led his horse to a forest. There he brushed him and groomed him well, and the horse shone as brightly as if he were made of gold. As he mounted the horses back, he took off into the sky like a bird and in no time they reached the Zmaj's palace. No sooner did the Tzar's son enter the palace, then he said to the Tzaritza:

'Get ready at once.'

She did, and they both mounted the horse and set off on their way. Not long after, the Zmaj returned to his palace and, seeing the Tzaritza gone again, said to his horse:

'Now what? Eat and drink or give chase?'

And the horse replied:

'Whether you eat or not, drink or not, chase or not—it is all the same. We shall never reach them.'

Hearing this, the Zmaj mounted his horse at once and gave chase. The Tzar's son and the Tzaritza, seeing the Zmaj right behind them, felt greatly affrighted and spurred their horse on, but the horse said to them:

'Fear not; there's no need to run.'

Not long after, the Zmaj nearly caught up with them and his horse called out to the Tzar's son's horse:

'For God's sake, my brother, slow down! I shall die trying to catch up with you thus!'

And his brother replied:

'But why are you so stupid to carry that monster? Fling your heels up in the air, throw him off to smash on the stones and come along!'

Hearing this, the Zmaj's horse shook his head and his body vigorously, flung his feet high up in the air and the Zmaj fell on the ground and smashed to smithereens; his horse then joined his brother for the Tzaritza to mount him. At last, they reached her Tzardom and lived there happily ever after.[5]

Notes

1. Drawn and quartered: a most severe punishment (often for high treason), where the convicted person would be tied to the tails of four horses who, spurred to gallop in four different directions, would tear the person apart.

2. Tzaritza [**tsah**-rit-suh], /ˈtsaˌrɪt sə/ (Serbian: Carica) is a wife of a Tzar; a Queen.

3. Brother-with-God is a close friend with whom one shares a bond so strong

55

they are like brothers (or sisters). This vow of mutual fidelity and trust once involved a ritual ceremony where their blood was mingled (hence the term blood brothers); in contemporary Serbian society this is no longer necessary; one can simply proclaim another his brother-with-God or sister-with-God.

4. In Serbian folklore, a witch is a woman (usually old) thought to have evil magic powers. She has an evil eye which she can cast over both people and animals; she is fond of attacking the young and live stock, and can cause illness, death, bad weather etc by use of her craft. Her usual mode of transport is a broom, but she can also shape-shift into a black bird, a moth or other winged creatures when she flies across the sky at night.

5. This tale contains motifs from at least two different Russian fairy tales: *Wassilissa the Beautiful* (the witch's house surrounded by human heads on display) and *Maria Morevna* (the shape-shifting mare, the unassuming horse who turns out to be a champion in disguise).

THE MAGIC RING

Once upon a time there lived a widow with an only son. She had nothing but a little house with a little plot of land where she grew plants and vegetables and, as she was unable to do heavy manual labour, they lived off this plot of land and off other people's charity. When the boy turned into a young man, he said to his mother:

'My dear mother, it is not fitting that we should beg and live off charity now that I am a strong and healthy youth; we should sell our plot of land and buy a horse and then I could fetch and sell timber and we could both live off this labour, instead of relying on other people's kindness.'

'O my dear child', his mother replied, 'if I were to sell the plot of land and buy a horse, you might not be able to look after the horse well in the woods and the wolves might devour him, and then we'll have neither the land nor the horse.'

But the son was insistent and kept pleading with his mother and eventually the mother gave in and let him sell the land to buy a horse. The young man then began fetching and selling timber, and they were able to survive from this labour just fine; although far from rich, they had enough to get by and did not lack food or fire.

One morning the mother asked the son to bring kindling, so that she could boil water and wash clothes. As usual, the son kissed his mother's hand and went into the woods. Once there, he left his horse grazing in a meadow, and went to collect kindling around the forest. Not long after, he heard a great clatter coming from the deep woods and ran to see what it was and where it was coming from. As he came to a clearing, he saw an extraordinary sight: an Aždaja had tried to swallow a deer and the deer's antlers got stuck in the Aždaja's mouth in such a way that it could neither swallow the deer in full nor spit it out, and so it squealed and howled in pain. Catching sight of the young man, she cried:

'Young man! I beseech you, in the name of God who sent you to me with that axe of yours as my brother, cut this deer's antlers and save me from my misery.'

And the deer said:

'Do not, in God's name do this; kill the Aždaja and save me instead.'

The youth pondered and weighed up his choices: if he were to attack the Aždaja, it could spit the deer out and devour the youth himself and, after all, it was the Aždaja who in God's name asked him first, so he decided to help the Aždaja. Quickly, he ran to the pair and struck the deer's antlers with his axe several times, until they came off, and the Aždaja devoured the deer in full.

Having devoured the deer thus, the Aždaja said to the young man:

'My brother-with-God, you saved me from my misery, and now it's my turn to pay you back. My father is the Tzar of Snakes and he will reward you handsomely; we should go to him now. But do not be fooled; refuse whatever else he offers you and ask for the ring.'

And so the Aždaja led the way, and the young man followed, deep into a cave. They walked through the cave and came out the other side and into a field which was teeming with snakes of all kinds. In the middle of the field there was a big table at the head of which the Snake Tzar sat. As they saw the Snake Tzar's daughter Aždaja, the snakes parted and made way for her—this calmed the young man somewhat, since he was greatly affrighted at the first sight of this field. As the Aždaja reached her father, she recounted to him all that had befallen her, and how the youth had saved her from her misery, and how she made him her brother-with-God and brought him to her father to reward him for his help. Hearing this, the Snake Tzar at once ordered his aides to prepare twenty loads of gold and riches for the young man but, to his surprise, the youth wouldn't even look at it and refused the gift with these words:

'I thank you, my Tzar, for these riches. If you wish to reward me, then give me the ring from your hand, and if you will not give me the ring, then I will take nothing else instead.'

The Tzar kept offering him whatever else he could think of, anything he wished save the ring, but the youth would not yield. At long last, the Tzar told him he would not give him the ring, for certain, so the youth bid them all farewell and turned to walk away. As the youth set off, the Tzar's daughter followed.

'Where are you going?', her father asked.

'What do you mean 'where'?', she replied. 'I am going away to roam around the world with my brother-with-God, since you would not reward him as he deserved to be rewarded.'

The Tzar felt sad to let his only daughter go like that, so he called them back and gave the young man the ring he wanted. Then the man and his sister-with-God Aždaja returned to the place where they had first met and she said to him:

'If you ever need anything, hold the ring close to an open flame, and your wish will be granted.'

So the youth left, with thoughts of his horse now stronger in his mind than the thought of the ring; but as he reached the spot where he had left the animal he found only the saddle and four horseshoes—the horse had been devoured by wolves. Crestfallen, he put the saddle on his own back and the horseshoes under his belt and, weary and worn out, reached his home at dusk. You'd think this would be the end of his troubles, but when his mother saw him coming back without the horse, and then when she found out it had been eaten by wolves, she chided and scolded him and even grabbed a stick and gave him a good beating. She then wouldn't give him any dinner, nor let him sleep in his room. Despondent, beaten and starving, the youth curled up in the corner and, all energy spent, fell asleep. He didn't sleep for long, however, as the rumble in his empty stomach got louder and louder and woke him up. It was only then that he remembered the ring, and held it next to the fire—at once, two Genies[1] appeared before him:

'Master, what is your wish?' they asked.

'I wish for food galore to be brought to me, this instant, and for the yard to be filled with timber and kindling, so that my mother can wash the clothes', he replied.

'Your wish is our command, master', they said; then they bowed out. His wish was fulfilled as requested, in the blink of an eye! He feasted on all sorts of delicacies to his heart's content, then he put some wood from the huge pile in the yard on the fire and fell asleep like a baby.

Next morning, his mother was up early—the thought of the lost horse and with it their livelihood didn't make for a good night's sleep. She stepped outside and, lo and behold!—the yard was full of timber and kindling. She went back inside to wake her son up and, seeing all the food around him, asked:

'What is all this, my son?'

'This, my mother, is what I got in exchange for the horse', he replied.

'Well, why didn't you tell me this last night, before I gave you such a beating?'

'I'm telling you now', he said, 'pray tell me, have I been forgiven?'

'You have, my son, you have', his mother said, showering him with hugs and kisses.

They went on living comfortably like that for some time, until one day the youth thought to himself:

'Why should we live in such a tiny little house?' Then he held the ring by the fire, and at once the two Genies appeared:

'What is your wish, master?'

'I wish for a palace fit for a Tzar to be built for me on a certain field, furnished with things fit for a Tzar, and when it's all done, for me and my mother to be moved there', he said. The Genies bowed out, and the youth and his mother went to sleep in their little house. In the morning, what should they see? His wish was fulfilled to his command, and he and his mother had been flown over to the palace without them even noticing. They made themselves at home there, and he told his mother not to let anyone hungry pass by the palace without being offered food, anyone thirsty without being offered water or anyone cold without being offered shoes and clothing. 'As God gave to us, so we shall share with the poor', he said.

One evening, sitting by himself, he thought:

'Indeed, as God gave to me thus, why should I be alone when I could get myself a wife to share my fortune with?' and so, pondering this thought, he brought the ring to the candle's flame. As always, the two Genies appeared before him at once:

'Your wish is our command, master!'

'I wish for a daughter of a Tzar or a Sultan[2], the most beautiful one, to be brought to me', he said. The Genies bowed out and, in the blink of an eye, they brought the Sultan's daughter. He welcomed her with open arms and caresses and gave her his heart; the maiden, seeing the riches equal to those in her father's palace thought he must be a Tzar himself or, at least, a Tzarevich of some kind, and so she returned his caresses; presently they married and lived happily together for some time.

When the Sultan noticed his daughter was missing, however, he began desperately searching for her, but could not find her anywhere—it was as if she had been swallowed up by the earth. Then he offered a big reward to whosoever could find her. The word of this reward reached an old witch-woman and so she went from town to town, from village to village, in search of the Sultan's daughter. She finally found her and went back to the Sultan to agree on the amount of riches she would get as reward for bringing his daughter back alive and well. Having agreed on the amount of reward with the Sultan, the witch took a cow hide of sorts and a staff, then set off on foot to reach the young man's palace. As he saw her approaching, our youth said to his wife:

'There's a poor old woman on the way, go tell my mother to invite her in and give her food and clothes.'

And his wife replied:

'Enough already with these poor old women!'

'I will have no-one pass by my house hungry and cold', he said. 'As God has given to me, so I shall give to the poor'.

The wife, as one should, listened to her husband and went to invite the old woman in, then asked her mother-in-law to go fetch some food and clothes for her. When the mother-in-law was gone, the witch said to the wife:

'Pray tell me, Sultan's daughter, does your husband make love to you?'

Astonished, the wife replied:

'Indeed he does; but I am mystified how you should know that I am the daughter of the Sultan.'

'How would I not know', said the witch, 'when I know everything there is to know? It was thanks to me that you were brought to marry this fine man. But, listen: go fetch that ring of his so I can cast a spell and have him make love to you ten times more.'

The wife was gullible and fell into this trap; she ran to her husband's room to fetch the ring. The husband, by his misfortune, was asleep; the wife carefully slipped the ring off his finger and replaced it with her own ring, then ran back to the witch. Grabbing hold of the ring, the witch said:

'Come hither, dear, and sit behind me on this hide!'

As the wife sat on the hide, the witch tapped it with the staff and they both took off. It is not a joke, my friends, a witch and her force—may she never cross our paths! They flew across the sky on the hide, until they reached the Sultan's palace and the witch exchanged his daughter for the agreed reward.

When our young man woke, he called to his wife; alas, to no avail. Then he called to his mother and asked after his wife, and the mother explained to him how the wife sent her to fetch food and clothes for the old woman he invited in, and by the time she was back both her daughter-in-law and the old woman were gone.

'Wherever she may be, I will find her', he said and reached for his ring, only to find it was his wife's ring on his finger. At once, he understood that he had been duped, and although this sudden realisation hit him like a ton of bricks he had no doubts of his wife's innocence. So he quickly disguised himself as a beggar and set off in search of her. In this manner he roamed the world for some time and, at long last, reached Istanbul[3]. He was at a loss as to how he could get a chance to meet his wife, so he went straight to the Sultan's palace and stood by the door. The Sultan's cook then arrived and, seeing him leaning on the door, asked him what he was waiting for. The young man replied:

'I have no work, so I'd like to join your kitchen, even just for food if not for wages—I can wash the dishes, at least.'

'All right then', said the cook, 'come inside, I'll give you work.'

So our young man settled in and in a few months time developed his skills and learned the trade and became the Sultan's cook's first assistant. Since he was a foreigner, and all the other cooks in the Sultan's kitchen local, they all went back home to sleep at night, and he stayed on his own in the kitchen. So as not to feel lonely, he got himself a cat and a dog to keep him company, and he looked after his animal friends well. There was also a slave-girl in the Sultan's palace who took the food from the kitchen to the harem[4], and he befriended her, too. One evening he said to her:

'My sister-with-God, I have a favour to ask you, if you can promise you will not tell another living soul about it.'

'My word is as solid as gold', she replied, 'tell me what's on your mind.'

'See this ring here?' he said, taking the ring off his hand. 'I shall put it inside this meal, which sits at the edge of the tray with food. Take this tray and offer this very meal to the Sultan's daughter, will you?'

'I will, my brother-with-God, have no doubt', the girl replied.

So he marked the plate clearly and the slave-girl took the tray and offered the meal with the ring inside it to the Sultan's daughter. The daughter began eating the meal, and with her second scoop picked up the ring in her spoon; recognising it at once (as it was her favourite piece of jewellery), she quickly hid it in her pocket. Later that evening, at bedtime, she summoned the slave-girl to her quarters and asked:

'You enter the kitchen every day; do you know if there is a foreigner working there?'

'There is', the slave-girl replied. 'He arrived some three or four months ago, the cook took pity on him but he learned the trade so well he is now the cook's first assistant.'

'And do you know where he sleeps at night?' the Sultan's daughter enquired further.

'I do; he sleeps in the kitchen.'

'And is there anybody else sleeping there beside him?'

'No, just his dog and his cat.'

'And do you happen to know anything about this ring?' the Sultan's daughter asked, taking the ring out of her pocket and showing it to the slave-girl.

The slave-girl smiled and said:

'Indeed, I do. He is a good and honest man, and he became my brother-with-God. He asked me to put the tray in front of you in such a way that you would naturally reach for the dish with the ring inside it, and he had me swear not to say a word to anybody about it.'

Hearing this, the Sultan's daughter said:

'And now I shall tell you a secret and you must promise me, too, that you will keep quiet about it, and no doubt you will also benefit from it.'

'My word is as solid as gold', the slave-girl vowed, 'tell me what's on your mind.'

'In that case, you should know that the man is my husband; go and take these dresses to him and bring him to my quarters, disguised as a woman.'

So the slave-girl took the clothes straight to the kitchen. When she recounted everything that had happened with the Sultan's daughter to him, our youth became as happy as a lark, over the moon. Quickly he put the dress on and, thus disguised as a woman, went by stealth to his wife's quarters. When they saw each other, they locked in each other's arms, the happiest two people in the whole

wide world; then once the initial wave of joy from this reunion had subsided, he asked his wife about his ring.

'I'm afraid that old woman took it', she replied, and recounted everything that had happened to her since.

'That is very bad news', he said, 'we will never be able to return to our home without it!'

'Well, we can always keep seeing each other in secret, like this, and thus live happily here', she responded.

And so it went. By day, he worked in the kitchen, by night he stayed with his wife. Not long after, however, through hear-say, the Sultan himself found out about this affair, and this knowledge caused him a great deal of anguish; after all, it was a great embarrassment that a Sultan's daughter should lie with a servant. So he went around looking for the culprit, questioning many and having many heads cut off, but to no avail—as those asked were unwilling to admit to something they were not guilty of. At long last, he summoned the old witch-woman and told her of his woes, and she replied to him thus:

'There is a foreigner working in your kitchen. He is the same man who took your daughter away; I recognised him straight away.'

The Sultan at once summoned his cook and demanded that the foreigner from the kitchen be brought to him. When the foreigner was brought to the Sultan, he was given a death sentence with no trial, no judge and no jury. And the witch said to the Sultan;

'My Sultan, pray give me two executioners, and I will have this man killed.'

The Sultan granted this wish to the witch, and so she took the young man to the mountains, accompanied by the executioners. There they found a big, deep hole in the ground and at the witch's command, the executioners pushed the man down the hole, then threw a great big boulder after him to seal his fate. As the man's cat and dog followed them all the way up the mountain, the witch had them thrown in the hole as well.

Luck favours the brave, and those who have God and luck on their side, cannot be harmed by humans. Our hero was one of those. After he was pushed down the hole, he didn't fall all the way down to the bottom, but managed to land on a protruding bit of rock half way down and hid in a cavity; the boulder hurled right past him and hit the ground. The cat and the dog followed not long after, but also managed to land on the protruding rock and climb into the cavity.

Now, however, the real trouble began: with no way out of the hole, and no sustenance inside. Our man spent a couple of days simply stroking his cat and his dog, conversing with them in his anguish. Then all of a sudden, they were gone; he couldn't feel them in the darkness that surrounded him. Now he really began to despair, but this did not last long; for the cat and the dog returned as they left, all of a sudden. As he stroked them, he noticed their bellies fool of food, and thought to himself:

'A-ha, they found something to eat somewhere; I must wait till they are hungry again and follow them in search of food.'

Not long after, the cat and the dog set off again, and he grabbed the dog's tail and followed it on all fours through the darkness. They didn't journey for long before they came out in some sort of clearing, teeming with mice and nothing else. As soon as they reached the clearing, the cat and the dog pounced on the mice, and the mice ran to their Tzar. Seeing the young man, the Tzar of Mice beseeched him:

'I implore you, my master, to hold back your army and I will give you whatever you may wish in return.'

The young man called to the dog and the cat and they obeyed and sat by his feet, and he said to the Tzar of Mice:

'I wish for nothing but the return of my ring from the hand of a certain old woman!'

The Tzar of Mice then summoned two of his more experienced subjects and sent them off on this quest; they didn't take long to return with over fifty rings of different shapes and sizes, all from the said old woman, but none of them happened to be his.

'My ring is not here', he said. 'Get my ring at once, or I shall send one of my soldiers to fetch a great army and unleash it on you.'

'There are no more rings in the old woman's possession', one of the two mice replied, 'bar one that she keeps under her tongue, so we cannot get hold of it.'

'I care not; you better bring me the ring here now, or I shall send for my army!' the young man threatened.

A small, weak mouse with a crooked leg then stepped forward, fearing that he'd be the first one to die in an army attack, and said:

'I shall go and get it, by God I will! Hold your army! Now, my Tzar, pray give me two strong, big comrades to carry me there and back, as I have a crooked leg and cannot go on my own.'

The Tzar assigned him two aides, and they set off and carried him all the way to the witch's house. The little mouse then went for a wee in the corner on top of a pile of rubbish, then brushed his tail in his wee and in the dust, saying to his comrades:

'As soon as I grab hold of the ring, you grab hold of me and run!'

Then he sneaked up to the witch, who was asleep on her belly, face down, and tickled her nostrils with his wet, dusty tail; the witch sneezed so hard she spat the ring out. The little mouse then grabbed the ring, and his comrades grabbed him and they quickly escaped before the witch had even realised what had happened.

When our hero saw the ring approaching, he was filled with joy; the only trouble was, there was no fire around, no open flame to bring the ring to. He pondered what to do and put his hands in his pockets: he was lucky again to find a couple of matchsticks there, he lit one and at once the two Genies appeared before him:

'Master, what is your wish?' they asked.

'I wish to be taken back into the light of the world, together with my cat and my dog', he said.

In the blink of an eye, they were up above, standing by the hole. He lit the second match and this time asked the Genies to bring the witch and to retrieve the boulder from the bottom of the hole; they pushed the witch down the hole first, then threw the boulder after her and 'bang!'—her fate was sealed forever.

He then took the ring and, relieved, returned to Istanbul. He stayed the night at an inn, and when everyone else was asleep, held the ring close to the fire; when his Genies appeared, he asked for his wife to be brought to him. Seeing him, she felt overcome with joy and with sorrow at the same time; joy at seeing him alive and well, sorrow for fear they would be discovered again and both be killed.

'Fear no more', he reassured her, 'I have my ring back.'

Then he recounted everything that had befallen him, and how he killed the witch and got his ring back. They stayed the night there, in peace and with joy, and in the morning he wouldn't go and hide; the servants recognised him and went straight to the Sultan. The Sultan took two executioners with him and went to have both his daughter and the man killed. Seeing the Sultan approach with his executioners, the young man quickly lit a matchstick and held his ring to it; then he had the Genies bring him four executioners to stand against the Sultan's two. Seeing this miracle, the Sultan called out to him:

'Hold back your executioners and I'll hold back mine; then we shall speak.'

This was exactly what the young man was hoping to hear, and so he held back his executioners and the Sultan came up to him and asked him who he was and where he had come from. He then told his story to the Sultan, just like I have told it to you, and then said:

'My dear lord, I have been fortunate and looked after by God so far, and your daughter loves me as much as I love her; we would like to have your blessing for our marriage.'

The Sultan thought for a short while, then said:

'So it was meant to be. I shall give you my blessing, on the condition that you stay here with me.'

'That is fine, my lord', the young man replied, 'I just need your permission to go and bring my mother here.'

The Sultan granted him this, and the young man brought his mother; the

Sultan then arranged a big celebration to mark their wedding.

If they are still alive to this day, they are still happy.[5]

Notes

1. A Genie is a spirit, from Arabic jinn (collective noun), as mentioned in the Qur'an and in Arabian folklore. The jinn inhabit the realm beyond the visible human realm and can be good, evil or neutral towards human beings. However, there is a significant difference in perception and interpretation of these creatures in Eastern and Western cultures. In the West, a genie is associated mainly with a wish-granting spirit, imprisoned in a bottle or oil lamp.

2. Sultan is a title given to a supreme ruler in Muslim countries, especially The Sultan—which relates to the Sultan of Turkey/ The Ottoman Empire.

3. Istanbul (previous names Byzantium, then Constantinopolis) is the largest city in Turkey, as well as one of the largest cities in Europe and in the world. Since its formation as Byzantium in 660 BC, it has been the country's economic and cultural centre, as well as one of the most significant cities in history and the capital of four empires: Roman Empire (330–395), the Byzantine Empire (395–1204 and 1261–1453), the Latin Empire (1204–1261), and the Ottoman Empire (1453–1922). It is the historic heart of the region and it was named a European Capital of Culture in 2010.

4. Harem comes from Arabic haram, which means 'forbidden or sacred place, sacrosanct'—it is the separate part of a Muslim household reserved for wives, concubines and female servants.

5. There is a similar story in Russian folklore, entitled *Martin the Peasant's Son*. However, whilst the tale here shares some of the main motifs (the magic ring, the cat and dog companions and the quest for the missing wife), the plot is very different and reflects not only the specifically Serbian tradition, but also the influence of the Ottoman Empire which ruled Serbia for 500 years. Although the first mention of a monarch relates to a Tzar, it quickly becomes the Sultan and numerous references to Turkish and Ottoman culture are made throughout the tale; of all the tales in this collection, The Magic Ring also has the largest number of Turkish words adopted into the Serbian language.

The Bear's Son

Once upon a time in a far-away village, women gathered to go up the mountain and collect herbs. As they roamed the mountain, one of them strayed from the group and came upon a cave. A bear came out of the cave, snatched her and married her. After some time had passed, she became pregnant and bore him a son.[1] One day, when the child had grown a bit, the woman managed to sneak out and run away back to her village and her home. The bear continued to bring whatever morsels he could find in the forest to feed the child, just as his mother did before she left. When the boy grew a bit older, he began pleading with his father to let him leave the cave in order to go out into the world and see what was there. His father, the Bear, would not consent to this, as he explained to the boy:

'You are too young still, and not strong enough. The world is full of wicked beasts called men, and they will kill you.'

So the boy was hushed for a while, and remained in the cave. But when some time had passed, the boy beseeched his father again to let him go out into the great wide world, and as the Bear had no other way to dissuade him, he took him out of the cave and under a beech tree.

'If you can pull this beech tree out of the ground,' he said to the boy, 'I will let you go; but if you cannot do this, then this will be a proof that you are too weak still and must remain with me.'

The boy pulled and pulled at the beech tree, but could not pull it out of the ground; so he returned to the cave with his father.

More time passed and again the child began to plead with his father to let him go, so the Bear brought him to the beech tree once more to see if he could pull it up by the roots. The boy pulled and pulled at the beech tree, and this time he pulled it out of the ground. The Bear then consented to let him go, and he had the boy cut the branches off the tree, so that he may use the trunk for a club. And so the boy set off on his journey, carrying the tree trunk over his shoulder.

69

One day, as the Bear's son travelled along the road, he came upon a field where hundreds of ploughmen were ploughing their master's land. He approached them and asked if they happened to have some food to share with him. They told him he should wait a little, their lunch was on its way, and where so many were eating, one mouth more mattered but little. As they spoke, the carts, the horses, the mules and the donkeys carrying their lunch appeared. When the food was laid out, the Bear's son declared how he could eat it all up by himself. The ploughmen marvelled greatly at his words, not believing it possible that one man could consume as great a quantity of food as would satisfy several hundred men. But the Bear's son insisted he could do it, and offered them a wager: if he did not eat it all up, he would give them his club, and if he did, they would have to give him all of the iron from their ploughs. No sooner was the lunch spread out than he pounced upon it and in a short time ate it all, so that not a crumb was left over and he could still have eaten seconds.

So the ploughmen gathered all their iron, and the Bear's son cut up a young birch tree, twisted it into a band and tied up the iron into a bundle, which he hung at the end of his club. Tossing this over his shoulder, he trudged away from the astonished and affrighted labourers. Going on a short distance, he arrived at a blacksmith's forge and requested to have a mace made from the iron he was carrying. This the smith undertook to do; but, putting aside half of the iron to keep for himself, he made of the rest a small, coarsely-finished mace.

The Bear's son saw at a glance that he had been cheated by the blacksmith and that the mace was much too small for all that iron; moreover, it displeased him to see such poor workmanship. So he decided to test it: he fastened the mace to the end of his club and threw it high up in the sky above the clouds, then got on all fours to catch the mace on his back. Unfortunately for the blacksmith, no sooner had the mace hit the Bear's son's back than it smashed to smithereens; the Bear's son grabbed his club and killed the blacksmith on the spot.

Having collected all of the iron hidden in the forge and the remains of the mace, the Bear's son then went to another blacksmith, and requested he made him a new mace, warning the blacksmith not to play tricks on him, but to use all of the iron and to make a fine mace, lest he should meet the same fate as the first blacksmith he went to. As the smith had heard what had happened to the other one, he gathered his apprentices, threw the iron in the fire, welded the whole together and forged a large mace with perfect workmanship. Again, to test it, the Bear's son fastened the new mace to the head of his club and threw it high up in the sky above the clouds, then caught it on his back. This time the mace did not break, but bounced. Then the Bear's son stood up and said:

'This is a fine mace!' and, tossing it over his shoulder, set off on the road. A little farther on he came to a field wherein a man was ploughing with two oxen, and he went up to him and asked for something to eat. The man said:

'I expect any minute now for my daughter to arrive with my lunch, then we shall share what God has given us!'

The Bear's son then told him how he had eaten up all of the food prepared for many hundreds of ploughmen, and asked:

'From a lunch prepared for one person how much can come to me or to you?'

Meanwhile the maiden brought the lunch. No sooner had she laid out the food, than the Bear's son reached for it and grabbed it, but the man held him back:

'No,' he said, 'you must first cross yourself and say grace, as I do!'

The Bear's son, hungry as he was, obeyed and, having said grace, they both began to eat. They ate until they'd had enough and there was still some leftover. The Bear's son, looking at the tall, strong, beautiful maiden who brought their lunch became very fond of her.

'Will you give me the hand of your daughter in marriage?' he asked the father.

'I would give her to you very gladly, but I have promised her already to Moustachio,' was the man's response.

'What do I care for Moustachio!?' the Bear's son exclaimed, 'I have my mace for him!'

'Now, now, Moustachio is also to be reckoned with!' the man replied. 'And he will be here any minute now.'

Not long after a noise came from afar, and lo! a moustache appeared behind a hill, and in it lay three hundred and sixty-five birds' nests. Bit-by-bit, the other moustache appeared, and then came Moustachio himself. Having reached them, he immediately lay down on the ground to rest. He put his head in the maiden's lap and told her to groom his head a little. The maiden did as he requested, while the Bear's son sneaked up behind him and struck him over the head with his mace. Whereupon Moustachio, pointing to the place with his finger, said:

'Something bit me here.'

The Bear's son then struck him with his mace on another spot and Moustachio, pointing to the place, said to the maiden:

'Something bit me again, right here!'

When he was struck a third time he said to the maiden angrily:

'Are you blind? Something bit me here!'

'Nothing bit you; a man struck you,' the maiden replied.

Hearing this, Moustachio sprang to his feet, but the Bear's son had thrown away his mace and was fleeing across the field. Moustachio pursued him, and although the Bear's son was lighter than he and had gained a considerable head start, Moustachio would not give up pursuing him.

The Bear's son, in the course of his flight, came to a river bank and nearby he found some men threshing wheat.

'Help me, my brothers, help—for God's sake!' he cried. 'Help! Moustachio is pursuing me! What am I to do? How can I get across this river?'

One of the men proffered his shovel, saying:

'Here, sit down on my shovel, and I will throw you over the river.'

The Bear's son sat on the shovel, and the man threw him over the water and onto the other bank; the Bear's son carried on running. Not long after, Moustachio came up, and asked the threshers if such and such a man had passed by there. The threshers replied that such a man had passed.

'How did he cross the river?' Moustachio asked.

'He leapt over,' they replied.

Moustachio then took a few steps back, ran and leapt over to the other bank, continuing to pursue the Bear's son.

Meanwhile, the latter, running hastily up a hill, began to grow tired and to slow down. At the top of the hill he found a man in a field sowing seeds. The sack with seeds was hanging from his neck, and after every handful of seeds sown in the ground, the man put a handful in his mouth and ate them. The Bear's son shouted to him:

'Help, my brother, help!—for God's sake! Moustachio is chasing me, and will soon catch up with me! Hide me somewhere!'

'Indeed, it is no joke to have Moustachio after you,' the man said. 'But I have nowhere to hide you, other than in this sack among the seeds.'

So he put the Bear's son in the sack. When Moustachio reached the sower he asked him if he had seen the Bear's son anywhere. The man replied:

'Yes, he passed by a long time ago, and God knows how far he has got to by now!'

Hearing this, Moustachio turned and went back whence he came. The man carried on sowing the seeds and, having forgotten all about the Bear's son in his sack, he scooped him up with a handful of seeds and put him in his mouth. The Bear's son, afraid of being swallowed, looked round the mouth quickly and, finding a hollow tooth, hid himself inside.

When the sower returned home in the evening, he called to his daughters-in-law:

'Children, give me my toothpick! There is something stuck in my broken tooth.'

The daughters-in-law brought him two long iron picks and, standing one on each side of him, they poked about with the two picks in his tooth until the Bear's son jumped out. Only then did the man remember him and said:

'That was not a good place to hide! I nearly swallowed you!'

Later on, after they had taken supper, they talked about many different things, and the Bear's son asked the man how come that one tooth was broken, whilst the others were all strong and healthy. And the man began spinning the yarn thus:

'Once upon a time myself and nine others set out with thirty horses for Dubrovnik[2] to buy some salt. As we journeyed on, we came upon a maiden in a field grazing her flock of sheep, and she asked us where we were bound for. We told her we were on our way to Dubrovnik to buy salt.

"Why go so far?" she said. "I have some salt in my bag, left over from feeding my sheep. I think it should be enough for you all."

So we agreed on the price, and she took the bag off her wrist, whilst we took the sacks from the thirty horses, and she poured the salt out of her bag, filling the sacks whilst we weighed them, 'til all the thirty sacks were full to the brim. We then settled our bill and turned to go back home. It happened to be a very fine autumn day, but as we were crossing the mountain Čemerno[3], the sky became overcast and snow came down, with cold winds from the north, and by the time we reached the summit of the mountain it became so pitch dark that we could not see our path; we wandered about here and there. At last, thankfully, one of us came upon a cave and called out:

"This way, brothers! I found a dry place!"

So we went in one after the other 'til we were all, with the thirty horses, safely under shelter. Then we unloaded the sacks from the horses, lit a fire, and passed the night there as if we were in a house. Next morning, just think what we saw! We were all inside a human head, which lay in the midst of some vineyards; and whilst we were still marvelling at this and loading our horses, the keeper of the vineyards came and picked the head up. He then put it in a sling and, swinging it about several times above his head, threw it and cast it far across the vines to frighten the starlings away from his grapes and the head with us all inside landed upon a hill. And that is how I broke my tooth.'

What a tall story![4]

Notes

1. According to Serbian folklore, bears used to be humans, turned into animals as punishment (for kneading the bread with their feet). St Andrew's day is celebrated 'because of the bears', and on this day the female bear is not mentioned by name but as 'she' or 'auntie'. Cornmeal gruel is made and left outside for her dinner. It is believed that a woman can conceive with a bear, and a man can have a child with a she-bear. In some parts, St Sava is also celebrated as a protector from bears.

2. Dubrovnik is a city on the coast of Adriatic Sea in Croatia.

3. Čemerno is a mountain in Western Serbia, near the town of Ivanjica (my home town), and also a mountain in Republika Srpska, Bosnia and Herzegovina.

4. Folklorists have identified The Bear's Son tale as a type of tale found in Europe, Asia and further afield in places such as Northern Mexico, British Columbia and Alaska. *Beowulf* is perhaps the best known European tale belonging to this group and there is a similar story in Russian folklore, entitled *The Little Bear's Son*. However, while the story here closely resembles the plot of the Russian version in the first half of the tale, after Mustachio's failed attempt at pursuing the Bear's son, the tale takes a very different, unexpected turn. My theory is that the narrator simply forgot what happened next but, as the tale was being written down for posterity by Vuk Stefanović Karadžić, he felt obligated to finish the story and so he made up the rest, creating, in the process, a brand new, truly fantastical tale.

VILA'S MOUNTAIN

Once upon a time there lived a rich man who had an only son. When the son came of age, his father sent him into the world to prosper, not by gaining riches but by gaining wisdom—he wanted his son to see how hard work could pay off, and how struggle was worthwhile in order to live one's life honestly, for the short time one had in this world. So he gave his son some money for the journey, and advised him to look after it well. With a blessing, he let the young man go.

Travelling the world far and wide, the young man came upon a town where he saw a man sentenced to death by hanging being led to the gallows. Astonished by this sight, he ran up to the executioner and asked what crime had the man been convicted of to deserve such a sentence? He was told that the man had owed money to many people and, as he was unable to pay back what he owed, by the laws of the town he deserved a death sentence. Hearing this, the young man asked the judge:

'My lord! Would it be possible to save this man from death by paying his debts off?'

'Why not!' the judge replied. 'Pay the amount he owes, and he is all yours.'

So the young man gave all the money he had, as well as his coat and outer garments. When the convicted man's debts were settled, he was released and handed over to the young man. The two of them then roamed the world together, begging for food. One night, as they lay side by side in a shelter, the saved convict said to the young man:

'I am tired of living like this; moreover, I am sad to see you struggle thus because of me. Let us go to the Vila's mountain, I have a sister-with-God there and she will give us advice on how to get rich.'

The young man agreed to this and so they set forth. They went along many byways and bridleways until they finally reached a mountain whose summit touched the moon, whose leaves were golden and whose trees were silver. A big flame burned in the midst of it. Seeing this, the young man felt alarmed and asked his companion:

'What is this? What sort of a wonder is this?'

'Fear not,' his companion replied. 'There are only my sisters-with-God here and their mothers, who are like our mothers. But we cannot turn up all of a sudden like this; I must go forth first and tell them we are here, and that we wish to stay with them. Wait for me there, under yonder tree made of pure gold with leaves made of pearls. But be careful not to let a sound out until I come back—that is the Vilas' tree, and they all gather under it in the Summer, embroidering; if they see a young man wandering around, they put a spell on him with a glance and turn him into whatever they wish.'

Having said this, the man disappeared as if he had been swallowed up by the earth.

The young man waited for his companion's return for some time and after a while, tired of waiting; so he began roaming the mountain and came upon a circle of winged maidens. He furtively drew nearer, to see them dance and hear them sing; by his misfortune, the leading maiden spotted him and at once put a spell on him so that he became blind and mute. The young man felt overcome with terror and began wailing and screaming, but at that moment his companion flew over and held him by the hand:

'What is it, what came over you?' he asked.

The young man gestured towards his eyes and his mouth. Seeing this, his companion took a kind of golden flute out of his pocket, climbed a tree and played the flute. At once, his brothers and sisters—all Vilas, and so many they could not be counted—appeared from all directions and flew about collecting various herbs from the mountain. Then they gave a potion to the young man to drink, and rubbed another potion on his eyes. He regained his sight, and his speech was ten times better than before. Vilas then accepted him into their company and had him married to one of them; he was rich and had many children. But towards his old age, he felt remorseful for his sins and decided to return to God and to his own home. His father was barely alive when he reached him, and he came in time to say goodbye and to bury him. After that he lived his life like a true Christian until he died. Except once every Summer, when he went back to Vila's mountain to see his company.[1]

Notes

1. This tale seems to embody the whole concept of Christianity attempting to take over pagan beliefs—and pagan beliefs stubbornly refusing to surrender and disappear.

The Tzar's Son-in-Law and The Winged Old Woman

Once upon a time there lived a young man who one night had a dream in which he married the Tzar's daughter. In the morning, he told his mother and father that he had just had a beautiful dream. But when his parents asked to hear more about this dream, the young man refused to tell them what it was about, and so they punished him for this insolence by throwing him out of the house and sending him away. He stood on the road crying for some time, when a Tzar's messenger came upon him.

'God help thee, my child!' said the messenger.

'God help thee!' replied the young man.

'How are you?' the messenger asked.

'I'm fine, thank you; and you?' said the young man.

'So why arc you crying then, if you are fine?' the messenger enquired.

And the young man responded:

'I had a beautiful dream last night, and my mother and father wanted to know about it and when I refused to tell them, they punished me and sent me away.'

'Well then', said the messenger, 'if you wouldn't tell them, you should tell me—I am a Tzar's envoy and I can tell the Tzar; if it is a good dream, good things may come your way.'

And the young man replied:

'Even if you were the Tzar himself, I would not tell you about my dream.'

Thence the messenger went to the Tzar and told him about his encounter with the young man. The Tzar then sent another envoy to find and bring the youth to him. The Tzar then asked him about his dream, but as the youth refused to tell, the Tzar threatened to have him hanged for his insolence, and the youth said:

'Though you may be the Tzar himself, I will not tell you of my dream.'

The Tzar then imprisoned him in a room within the confines of his palace. This room happened to be right next to the room where the Tzar was keeping his daughter safe from the world, until she came of age. In the evening, as the poor youth sat imprisoned, wondering what to do, he heard the clinking of cutlery and crockery coming through the wall of his cell. He then felt around the wall looking for a weak spot and, finding one, dug through and peered into the adjacent room. And what was he to see there?—but the Tzar's daughter, asleep, with her maids sleeping around her! A mottled candle burned above her head, and a white one by her feet; on the table in front of them, a big feast was laid out. Slowly, carefully, he sneaked through the hole in the wall and into the room; then feasted on the leftovers of food and drink and swapped the two candles: he put the motley one by the Tzar's daughter's feet, and the white one by her head. Then he sneaked back into his own cell and repaired the wall so skilfully, no-one would ever be able to tell it had been tampered with. Next morning, when the Tzar's daughter woke, she saw the candles had been swapped and the table emptied of food; she chided her maids angrily, certain it was them who had done this. The maids swore how they were not to blame for this strange occurrence, but the Tzar's daughter still remained suspicious of them. She sent a letter to her father, telling him of the intruder who had come during the night to eat and drink from her table and also asking him to forbid the maids from switching her candles over. The Tzar did as she asked. In order to catch the intruder in her sleep, she rubbed a herbal tincture on her eyelids—this was a potent herb which could give dream visions; then she went to bed after dinner. In the small hours of the night, our youth dug through the wall again and entered the Tzar's daughter's room. He ate and drank whatever he found on the table, then took the mottled candle from above the Tzar's daughter's head and placed it by her feet, and took the white one by her feet and placed it next to her head. As he turned to go back to his cell, the Tzar's daughter grabbed him by the arm and, seeing what a handsome youth he was, she began to question him: she wanted to know who he was and where he had come from and why he had been imprisoned by her father. She then let him go. The following morning, she sent a letter to her father asking him to send more food and drink to her room, for her maids were always hungry. The Tzar did as she asked, and from then on, our youth kept re-visiting the Tzar's beautiful daughter at night, feasting at her table and spending the night with her. Then, one day, the Tzar issued a decree announcing that his daughter was old enough to marry. Hearing this, the Tzar's daughter informed him how she only intended to marry the one who could throw a spear over the walls of the Tzar's city. The Tzar summoned all his noblemen and ordered them to bring their sons to the Tzar's palace the following Friday. They did as they were told, and on the given day the Tzar brought his daughter out and held a spear as she requested, announcing how the young man who wished to become the Tzar's son-in-law must throw the spear over the city walls. The suitors all strived to accomplish this task; alas, none succeeded. Seeing this, the Tzar's daughter then asked her father to have the prisoner from the tower brought out to try his hand at this challenge as well—the one imprisoned three years earlier, whom she could hear breathing on the other side of the wall of her room. The Tzar was astonished to hear this; he had all but forgotten about this prisoner, believing him to be long dead in his cell. He had the youth brought out and was further astounded to see him looking so well; he liked him a lot at first sight. He then handed the spear to the youth and asked him to throw it over the walls. The noblemen and their sons all laughed at this and mocked the young man:

'Ha, ha, indeed, this miserable wretch should throw the spear over the wall, and the sons of Mohammed[1] could not!'

But their mockery was short-lived: the youth cast the spear over the walls and thirty feet farther, where it sank half-way down into a boulder. Seeing the great skill of the young man, the Tzar cared not about his lowly background and his being a prisoner; he made the youth an officer in his army and offered him his beautiful daughter's hand in marriage, as well as plenty of gold and riches. The noblemen's sons were very envious of this, and so they conspired to have the Tzar's daughter taken away from him. They offered the Tzar's son-in-law a wager: the following Friday, the noblemen's sons were to prepare a feast big enough for a thousand souls, and the Tzar's son-in-law was to bring his wife and a thousand people to try and eat it all up; should they fail to finish the feast, the Tzar's son-in-law was to hand over his wife and his whole entourage to them. Both parties agreed to this wager in writing. When the time came, the Tzar's son-in-law gathered his company; however, they counted only nine hundred and ninety five people. Nonetheless, the Tzar's son-in-law set off with them, together with his wife.

Along the way, they came upon a man lying with his ear pressed to the ground. The Tzar's son-in-law greeted him:

'God help thee, my brother!'

'God help thee!' the man replied.

'What are you up to?' the Tzar's son enquired.

'Nothing much; just listening to the grass grow.'

Hearing this, the Tzar's son-in-law offered to the man:

'Would you like to join my company, then, since you are not doing very much? The noblemen's sons have invited me to a feast; you will enjoy this.'

The man accepted this kind offer, and so the Tzar's son-in-law gained his nine hundred and ninety sixth companion.

A little further on, they came upon another man, standing still in the middle of the road, looking intently around and checking in all the directions. The Tzar's son enquired what he was up to and what he was waiting for and the man said:

'I made a wager with a bird to see which one of us was faster: I was to run and the bird was to fly; it has been three hours now since I arrived here, and the bird is nowhere in sight.'

Astounded to hear of such great speed, the Tzar's son-in-law asked the man:

'Would you care to join us, brother? The noblemen's sons have invited me to a feast; you too will enjoy this.'

The man agreed, and so the Tzar's son-in-law gained his nine hundred and ninety seventh companion.

Still further on, they came upon a third man, staring intently into the sky. The Tzar's son-in-law asked him why he was staring into the sky in such a way and what was he expecting to see there. The man replied:

'I threw a spear up into the heavens, and I have been waiting for it to come back down for the past three hours.'

The Tzar's son-in-law invited this man along, too; the man joined them and became the nine hundred and ninety eighth companion.

As the company journeyed on, after about an hour they saw a man by the side of the road who had cooked up sixty stone of corn gruel in a huge cauldron for his breakfast and had eaten it all up; he was still hungry so he scraped the sides of the cauldron with his spoon. The Tzar's son-in-law greeted him and asked:

'What are you doing, brother?'

'Well,' the man replied, 'I made some breakfast earlier on, and could easily eat seconds, if only there was any food left in here.'

The Tzar's son-in-law asked this man, too, to join them, as they were on their way to a big feast; the man was only too happy to do so and the company now counted nine hundred and ninety nine men.

Continuing their journey, they came upon a fifth man: he had drank up a whole lake and was standing over its empty basin, watching the fish flapping about on dry ground. The Tzar's son-in-law greeted him and asked what he was up to.

'Nothing much,' replied the man. 'I had some breakfast this morning and stopped here afterwards to wash it down with water; I'm just looking at these little fish flapping about on dry land.'

This man, too was asked to join the company; he did and the Tzar's son-in-law now had an entourage one thousand-strong.

When they arrived at the agreed place, they dismounted their horses and rested for a short while. The noblemen's sons had prepared an impressive feast: food and drink galore, enough for four thousand souls. The Tzar's son then sent the man who had eaten sixty stone of corn gruel for breakfast and was still hungry to go and have a little taste of the feast for them. The man went and tasted one thing after another, a little bite from here, a little scoop from there, until he licked all the pots and the plates clean. He then went and drank all there was to drink too, and returned to the Tzar's son-in-law informing him how he had eaten up the entire feast and wouldn't mind having some more. Hearing this, the Tzar's son-in-law called the noblemen's sons and asked them to give him their wives. They implored him not to take their wives over this first wager, and offered him another one; should the Tzar's son-in-law win this wager too, they would give him their wives and all their land. The Tzar's son-in-law agreed to this and the bet was on: the noblemen's sons were to light a big furnace and the Tzar's son-in-law was to send one of his men into the fire; should he succeed in surviving the heat, they would hand over their wives and their land; should he burn to death, the Tzar's son-in-law was to hand over his wife and his whole entourage to them. When the furnace was lit and ready, the Tzar's son-in-law asked the man who had drunk the entire lake to go and jump into the fire. The man went in and immediately regurgitated all the lake water and put the fire out. He then sang triumphantly:

'The Tzar's son-in-law will now have four wives! We won the bet, we won, indeed!'

Seeing that this second wager did them no good either, the noblemen's sons felt greatly affrighted and so they begged the Tzar's son-in-law to agree to have one last bet. They had with them a winged old woman, and they asked the Tzar's son-in-law to pick one of his men to race this woman to a certain mountain to fetch water from a certain spring; whichever one of the two returned with the water first would be the winner of this last wager. The Tzar's son-in-law then summoned the man who had raced with a bird and had waited for three whole hours at the finish line for the bird to arrive. The noblemen gave this man and the winged old woman a vessel each; they took off. The man reached the spring first and filled his vessel with water. No sooner did he fill the vessel, however, than the winged old woman appeared, snatched this full vessel and swapped it with her empty one, then quickly flew back. By the time the man had filled the empty vessel, the old woman was far ahead of him. But the man who could hear the grass grow picked up on the sound of her wings flapping and ran to the Tzar's son-in-law with the news:

'The winged old woman tricked our man and took his full vessel, leaving her empty one in his hands; by the time he filled the empty vessel, she gained quite an advantage and is almost here now—I can hear her wings.'

Hearing this, the Tzar's son-in-law called the man who had cast the spear into the sky and waited for three whole hours for it to come down; this man spotted the winged old woman in flight and threw a spear at her, striking her right in the chest. The winged old woman dropped dead on the ground, and in that moment the other man arrived with the water.

So the Tzar's son-in-law took the three noblemen's wives and all their possessions and returned to his palace with his wife and all his company, where he lived happily for the rest of his days.

Notes

1. Although the supreme ruler in this tale is a Tzar rather than a Sultan, 'sons of Mohammed' denotes that the noblemen were Ottoman. Thus, this tale is a good example of a typically Balkan mix of cultures, the Slavic and the Turkish influences interchange throughout (see also: The Magic Ring, Note 1).

The Golden-fleeced Ram

Once upon a time there lived a hunter who oft went up the mountain looking for game. One day as he went a-hunting, he came across a golden-fleeced ram[1]. As soon as he saw the ram, the hunter reached for his rifle to shoot him down, but the ram was faster and he charged at the hunter and stabbed him with his horns. The hunter dropped dead on the spot, and when his companions had found his body, they picked him up and carried him home to bury him, not knowing who was to blame for his death. The hunter's widow then hung his rifle upon a nail above the door. When her little son turned into a young man, he asked his mother to give him the rifle to go hunting in the mountains, and the mother would not consent to this request. She spoke to him thus:

'My dear son, I shall not let you have this rifle, never, under any circumstances! Your father lost his life with this rifle, would you have the same happen to you?'

One day the young man decided to take the rifle anyway, by stealth, and he went a-hunting. As he came upon a clearing in the forest, the same golden-fleeced ram appeared before him and said:

'I killed your father, and now I shall kill you, too.'

And the young man trembled and said:

'God help me!' then shot his rifle and killed the ram. He rejoiced at having killed a golden-fleeced ram that couldn't be found in the whole Tzardom, and he skinned it and took its golden fleece back home with him. Not long after, the word of his feat spread across the Tzardom and reached the Tzar himself, and the Tzar demanded that the fleece be brought to him so that he could see what sort of animals lived in his Tzardom.

When the young man brought the fleece to the Tzar, the Tzar said to him:

'Ask what you wish in exchange for this fleece.'

And the young man replied to the Tzar:

'Offer what you will, I shall not part with it.'

One of the Tzar's attendants happened to be an uncle of the young man, and this uncle was not the young man's friend, but his enemy. He said to the Tzar:

'Since he won't give you the fleece, we should get rid of him; ask of him to do such a thing as cannot be done.'

So the young man was summoned and the Tzar ordered him to plant a vineyard and within a week to come back and bring wine from this vineyard. Hearing this the young man began to weep and to plead with the Tzar not to demand such a thing of him as cannot be done, but the Tzar responded thus:

'Should you fail to return within a week with the wine from this vineyard, you shall be executed.'

Then the young man went back home and told his mother what had happened and the mother, hearing this, exclaimed:

'Haven't I told you, my son, that the rifle will cost you your life, just like it did to your father?'

So the young man walked away in tears, wishing he were dead, and when he had walked for a good while and had reached a good distance away from his village, a maiden appeared before him and asked him why he was in tears. The young man replied angrily:

'Be off with you, since you cannot help me!' and walked on, but the maiden followed him and beseeched him to confide in her.

'For all you know', she said, 'I might well be able to help you'. Then the young man paused and spoke to her thus:

' I shall tell you, though none bar God himself may be able to come to my aid.'

Then he recounted all that had befallen him, and what the Tzar had demanded of him. Hearing this, the maiden said:

'Fear not, my brother, but go and ask the Tzar to tell you where your vineyard should be and to have this land marked and chartered, and then put a bunch of basil[2] in a bag, and go and sleep on the marked spot, and in a week's time your grapes will be ripe.'

The young man then returned home and in despair told his mother of his encounter with the maiden and of her words. Hearing this, his mother advised him thus:

'Go, my son, and follow her advice; there is nothing else for you to do.'

The son went and asked the Tzar to mark the plot of land for his vineyard, and the Tzar had everything done as the young man had requested. The young man then took a bag with a bunch of basil in it and, feeling dismayed, lay on the marked ground to sleep. When he woke the next morning, the vineyard was planted; the day after, it sprouted leaves, and in a week the grapes were ripe and ready—even at this time, well out of the grape season! He picked the grapes, crushed and pressed them and made sweet wine, then took it to the Tzar, together with some fresh grapes wrapped in a scarf. The Tzar was astounded to see this, as

84

were all his attendants. Then the young man's uncle said to the Tzar:

'Now we shall ask of him something else, something that truly cannot be done.' So he gave counsel to the Tzar, and the Tzar summoned the young man and ordered:

'You shall make me an ivory city.'

Hearing this, the young man walked away in tears and recounted to his mother the Tzar's latest demand, saying:

'This, my mother, I truly cannot do, nor can it be done.'

And his mother replied:

'Go, my son, for a walk outside the village; perhaps you will come upon the maiden again.'

He walked away from the village, and when he reached the spot where he had met the maiden for the first time, there she was again, and she spoke to him:

'My brother, you are sad and miserable again.'

And so he told her all about the latest request the Tzar had placed upon him, and she advised him thus:

'This will be easy, too; go to the Tzar and ask for a ship with 300 litres of wine and 300 litres of rakija[3] and also for 12 carpenters aboard the ship. Sail out on this ship, and when you reach the place where there is a gorge between two mountains and a stream at the foot of the gorge, build a dam over the waters and pour all the wine and rakija in it. Elephants will come to drink water there, and they will become drunken from all the wine and rakija and fall to the ground in a haze; get the carpenters then to cut off their tusks and take the tusks to the plot of land the Tzar had marked for the city, then lie down and go to sleep, and in a weeks' time your city will be made.'

Thus advised by the maiden, the young men returned home and recounted everything to his mother, and the mother said to him:

'Go, my son, and perhaps you will be helped once more.'

The son went to the Tzar and made his requests, then did everything as the maiden had advised him: elephants did indeed come to drink and did fall to the ground in a haze, and the carpenters did cut their tusks off and took them to the allotted plot of land; in the evening, the young man put a bunch of basil in a bag and went to sleep on the spot and in a weeks' time the ivory city was built.

When the Tzar saw the beautiful city, he was deeply astonished and he said to his attendant, the young man's uncle:

'What am I to do? This is not a man we see before us, this is something else.'

And the attendant replied:

'There is one more task you should give him, and should he accomplish this too, then he truly is more than a man.'

And so he gave his counsel to the Tzar, and the Tzar summoned the young man once more:

'Now you shall bring me the daughter of a certain Tzar, from a certain Tzardom', he demanded, 'and should you fail to accomplish this, I shall have you beheaded.'

Hearing this, the young man returned home and told his mother of this latest demand put upon him, and the mother replied:

'Go, my son, and look for the maiden again; Godspeed, you will be helped once more!'

And so he ventured out of the town, and found the maiden and recounted everything to her, and the maiden advised him thus:

'Go and ask the Tzar for a galley-ship, and for it to have twenty shops inside, and each of the shops to have different goods of the highest quality in stock, each one better than the last, and for the finest young men dressed in the finest clothes to be attending these shops as merchants. Then you shall board this galley and you will meet, firstly, a man carrying a white-tailed eagle, and you shall ask him to sell you the bird; he will say yes, and you shall give him whatever he desires in return. Then you will meet another man, carrying a golden-scaled carp in a canoe; buy this golden carp at any price. Then you will meet a third man, carrying a pigeon; buy the pigeon, too, at any cost. Pull one feather from the eagle's tail, and the scales from the carp, and a single feather from the pigeon's left wing; then let them all go. When you reach the other Tzardom, open all the shops and have all the merchants stand in front of their own. Then all the townsfolk shall gather in wonderment, and all the maidens shall say:

'Since the beginning of this town, there never has been a finer galley, nor a finer market.' The word will then reach the Tzar's daughter, and she will beseech her father to let her see this wonder. When she comes aboard the galley with her companions, you shall take her from one shop to the next, show her all the finest goods, and keep her entertained until dusk; as the dusk falls, you shall start the galley, and in that very same moment deep darkness will descend upon the Tzar's town. The Tzar's daughter, as always, will have a bird upon her shoulder, and as soon as the galley is on the move, she will send the bird to her father's palace with the news of her demise. You shall then light the eagle's feather with a match and as soon as you do this, the eagle will appear before you and you shall send him to catch the bird. Next, the Tzar's daughter will throw a pebble in the waters, and the galley will come to a halt immediately; you shall take the carp's golden scales and set them on fire, and in that moment the carp will come to you, and you shall send him to find and swallow the pebble, and as soon as he does this, the galley will be on the move once more. Thenceforth, you will have a long and pleasant journey, until you reach a ravine between two mountains: there your galley will turn to stone, and you will all be struck with terror; the maiden will then demand you bring the mystic live water4 to her, and you shall set the pigeon's feather on fire, which will bring the pigeon to you at once—you shall give him a vessel and he will bring you the live water; the galley will then be on the move again and you will finally reach your home in peace, with the Tzar's daughter aboard the ship.'

Having heard all this, the young man returned home and recounted everything to his mother, before going to the Tzar with his requests. The Tzar had no choice but to grant him his requests, and so the young man set off on his galley. Along the way, everything occurred as the maiden had predicted and he did all as he was told; he reached the other Tzardom and got hold of the Tzar's daughter and followed all the advice he was given. At length he returned home. The Tzar and his aide watched them arrive from the palace windows, and the aide said to the Tzar:

'Now you shall have his head cut off as soon as he steps one foot on the shore, there is nothing else left for you to do.'

As the galley reached the shore, all its passengers alighted, first the Tzar's daughter with her companions, then the handsome merchants, and finally the young man; no sooner did he step one foot on the ground, than the Tzar's executioner cut his head off. The Tzar was intent on taking the other Tzar's daughter for himself, and as soon as she alighted, he leapt over to her and began to fawn on her, but she turned away from him and asked:

'Where is the one who went through all that trouble for me?' and seeing him beheaded on the ground, she grabbed the live water and poured it over him, and his head was joined with his body once more and he was instantly brought back to life. Seeing him alive and well again, the aide said to the Tzar:

'Now he will be even more knowing, since he has been dead and resurrected.'

The Tzar then wished to find out whether one truly knew more when one came back from the dead, and so he demanded that his head be cut off, too, and that the Tzar's daughter pour live water on him afterwards. The Tzar was then beheaded, but the maiden wouldn't even look at him; instead, she at once wrote a letter to her father, recounting all the events that had happened and admitting how she wanted to marry the young man who took her away. Her father replied asking the people of that Tzardom to accept the young man as their new Tzar, lest he send an army at them. The people of the Tzardom accepted the young man as their new Tzar as it was only right. So our young man married the Tzar's daughter and became a Tzar, and all the merchants that accompanied him on journey married his wife's companions and became noble squires.4

Notes

1. In Serbian folklore, a ram is a symbol of strength, and the golde

symbol of wealth and wisdom. As it is considered to be a blessed animal, it is often offered as sacrifice (at weddings, family patron saint days etc). It is believed that sheep can foretell the weather and restore good health. Saint Sava is the patron saint of sheep.

2. According to Serbian folklore, basil is a plant with mystical powers, able to protect from evil eyes and witchcraft—for this reason it is placed on the pillow next to a newborn child. It is believed to have special powers when it comes to love and fertility, and is often used in love-affirming rituals.

3. Rakija [**ra**-khy-ya], /'răkija/ is a spirit, a strong alcoholic drink made by distillation of various types of fruit; plum rakija or šljivovica [**shilli**-vo-vitza], /'ʃʎivovitsa/ is the most popular and considered the national drink of Serbia. Rakija is also made from apricots, pears, grapes, cherries, quince and other fruit and is a popular national drink across the Balkan countries.

4. This tale could be seen as the Serbian version of the Ancient Greek myth featuring Jason and the Argonauts: the motifs of golden fleece, the quest and the ascension to the throne are all there. The plot is very different, however, abundant with typically Slavic elements of folklore and set in the Serbian landscape. While there are numerous interpretations of the golden fleece motif in relation to the Greek myth, here it seems to clearly represent royal power, wealth, kingship and, perhaps, God's favour/ protection.

The Snake Bridegroom

Once upon a time there lived a Tzaritza who was childless and she prayed to God each day to let her have a child, even if it were a snake. Not long after, she gave birth to a snake. She looked after and nourished the snake as any mother does with her newborn. In twenty two years, the snake never said a word; when he was twenty two years old, he suddenly said to his parents:

'I am ready to marry.'

His parents replied:

'Who could give their daughter to a snake? Which maiden would marry a snake?'

'Well,' the snake replied, 'you should not look for a Tzar's daughter or a nobleman's daughter, but for a maiden who would be happy to marry a Tzar.'

His parents then told him to go and find a maiden for himself. The snake did this, found a maiden who was poor and sent his father to ask for her hand. The maiden was delighted and happily agreed to marry a snake, since she was so poor. The groom's father then brought her to his son, and the couple were married and lived happily thus for some time. Eventually, the wife became pregnant. Hearing the news of her bearing a child, her mother-in-law asked:

'How on earth did you manage to get pregnant with a snake, my child?'

The wife was reluctant to tell her about it, but the mother-in-law was insistent and kept asking her the same question for several days in a row. At last, the wife confessed that her husband was not actually a snake, but a young man so handsome he had no rival in the whole wide world.

'By day, he is a snake,' she said. 'But at night, as soon as it gets dark, he sheds his skin[1] to reveal a beautiful young man. Ah, how I wish he could be the same during the day as he is at night; alas, at the crack of dawn he puts his snakeskin back on and becomes a snake again.'

The mother-in-law was overcome with joy at hearing all this, and she said her daughter-in-law:

'Right, we shall then make him stay permanently the way he is at night.'

She then advised the wife thus:

'When your husband sheds his skin in the evening and, as usual, puts it under his pillow, you should wait for him to fall asleep then take the skin from under the pillow and pass it to me through the window.'

The wife did as she was advised, stole the skin and passed it over to her mother-in-law who was waiting under their bedroom window. The mother-in-law took the skin and cast it into the fire. No sooner had the skin caught fire however, than the husband jumped from his slumber and shouted:

'What in God's name have you done? Now you see me; and you shall see me next when you have worn out iron shoes while searching for me and your iron cane has crumbled to dust. The child that you carry in your belly shall not see the light of day until I have put my arm around you again.'

With these words, he disappeared.

Three years later, his wife was still pregnant with their child and, at long last, feeling forlorn, she decided to go and look for her husband. So she made iron shoes and an iron cane for her journey, and she set out. Roaming the world thus, she came across the mother of the Sun, who was lighting fire in her furnace, turning the embers with her bare hands. Seeing this, the wife quickly ripped a piece of her skirt and wrapped it around the hands of the mother of the Sun. The mother of the Sun asked her:

'What brings you here, Christian soul?'

And the wife replied:

'Misery brings me here, my mother.' Then she told the mother of the Sun everything that had befallen her, and how her husband put a curse on her so she must roam the world in search of him.

'I came to ask your son if he could shed some light on this matter and tell me something about my husbands whereabouts, since your son travels the world each day and may have seen him somewhere.'

The mother of the Sun was very sad to hear this and she said to the woman:

'Here comes my son the Sun[2]; it would be best for you to hide behind the door for a minute, as he may come back tired and angered by the clouds, he may harm you in some way in his anger. Best to let him rest for a short while first.'

The wife hid behind the door as the Sun entered.

'Good evening, my mother!' he greeted from the door. 'There is a Christian oul in this house, I can smell it.'

'No, there isn't,' his mother replied. 'Not even a bird can fly up here, how would uman manage to reach this place?'

'here is a human in here, mother,' the Sun said. 'Let her come out and show lf, I won't harm her.'

So the woman came out from behind the door, and told her woes to the Sun.

'O brilliant Sun,' she said, 'you shine all over the world; have you, perhaps, noticed a man of such description as my husband?'

The Sun replied that he hadn't seen such a man in the daytime, but perhaps the Moon[3] might have seen him at night; so he told the woman to go and ask the Moon. On her departure, the mother of the Sun gave her a golden distaff with golden wool and golden spindle.

As the woman reached the house of the Moon, she found his mother there; she kissed her hand and greeted her:

'God help thee, mother of the Moon!'

'God help thee, Christian soul!' the mother of the Moon replied. 'What brings you here?'

The woman recounted everything that had befallen her to the mother of the Moon; told her how she went to see the mother of the Sun and showed her the present she was given. She also explained how the Sun told her to ask the Moon if he had seen her husband at night somewhere. The mother of the Moon advised her to hide behind the door for a little while, since the Moon was on his way back, tired and angry. The woman stood behind the door, and at that moment the Moon appeared.

'Good morning, my mother!' he called from the door. 'There is a Christian soul in here, I can smell it.'

'No, there isn't,' his mother replied. 'Not even a bird can fly up here, how would a human manage to reach this place?'

'There is a human in here, my mother, there is,' the Moon insisted. 'But let her come out and show herself, I will not do her any harm.'

The woman then came out and told the Moon all her woes. Then she asked;

'O radiant Moon, you shine all night across the great wide world, have you happened to see my husband anywhere?'

And the Moon replied:

'I haven't seen your husband anywhere at night, Christian soul; but you should go to the Wind[4] and ask him if he had seen your husband somewhere, since the Wind gets everywhere and slips through all the nooks and crannies.'

On her departure, the mother of the Moon gave her a golden hen and chicks.

Thence, the woman continued her quest. She found the mother of the Wind and told her all that had befallen her, then asked if the Wind might know something.

'Stand behind the door for a moment,' the mother of the Wind said to her. 'My son will be back shortly, and he may be angry.'

The woman stood behind the door; anon, the Wind appeared, howling, blowing, breaking and knocking things over.

'God help thee, mother!' he shouted from the door. 'I can smell a Christian soul in here.'

'God help thee, my son, ' his mother replied. 'But there are no Christian souls in here; a bird couldn't fly up here, and how would a human manage to reach this place?'

'There is a human here, my mother, there is,' the Wind replied. 'Let her come out and show herself, I will not do her any harm.'

So the woman came out in the open, and told the Wind all about her woes. The Wind said to her:

'I have seen your husband, indeed—in a far, far away Tzardom. He has re-married and he is the Tzar. Now, my mother shall give you a golden loom, with golden yarn and golden spindle. When you get to the Tzar's town, place your loom outside the Tzar's palace and start weaving; also let the hen and her chicks out to peck, and have your distaff out on display, too.

The woman thanked the Wind for his advice and set off. As she reached the Tzar's town, her shoes fell off her feet, all worn out, and her cane broke in half. She set the loom outside the Tzar's palace, let the hen and the chicks out and took her distaff, then began to weave. The Tzaritza spotted her weaving from her window, and thought to herself: 'By God, I am a Tzaritza and I don't have a golden loom and distaff, nor a golden hen and chicks.' So she sent her servant to go and ask the woman if she would sell these golden possessions. The woman replied:

'I shall not sell a thing, but if the Tzaritza lets me spend a night with her husband the Tzar, I shall give her my distaff.'

The Tzaritza agreed to this. However, she secretly fed magic herbs to her husband; no sooner had his head touched the pillow, than he fell into a deep slumber. As the woman entered his room, she beseeched him:

'My honourable Tzar, my shining light, will you please put your right arm around me so that I can give birth to this child of yours.'

But the Tzar did not stir and slept on, as if he were dead.

The following day, the woman gave the Tzaritza the golden distaff and the golden yarn. The Tzaritza then asked for the hen and the chicks, too. The woman promised to give them to the Tzaritza, should she be allowed another night alone with the Tzar. The Tzaritza, of course, agreed to this and did the same as before— secretly she charmed her husband so that he would sleep without waking all night. The woman went to his room and begged him from the top of her voice:

'My honourable Tzar, my shining light, will you please put your right arm around me so that I can give birth to this child of yours!'

But the Tzar did not stir.

In the morning, when he woke, the guards told him about the woman who came to his chambers for two nights in a row, and how she beseeched him to put his right arm around her, so that she could give birth to their child.

When the Tzaritza received the golden hen and chicks, she asked for the loom and the spindle, too. The woman promised to give these things to the Tzaritza, should she be allowed one last night alone with the Tzar. The Tzaritza agreed to this, intending to bewitch her husband again. But the Tzar, having heard the guards' story of the woman who visited him at night, took a sponge and put it under his chin. When the Tzaritza brought him a drink at bedtime, he poured it onto the sponge without drinking a sip and pretended he was asleep. As the woman came into his room, she beseeched him:

'My honourable Tzar, my shining light, will you please put your right arm around me so that I can give birth to this child of yours!'

Hearing this, the Tzar put his right arm around her at once; she went into labour that very same moment and gave birth to a boy with golden hair and golden arms. The Tzar then left his new Tzardom and his Tzaritza, and returned home with his first wife and their child.[5]

Notes

1. Snakes moult in the Spring, by rubbing against stones or bushes. It is believed that the person who finds a snake's shed skin on St George's day will be very fortunate all year. The shed skin is also worn as an amulet, and it is believed that it can be used both to prevent and to treat illness in live stock.

2. In Serbian folklore, the Sun is a living being. Although its gender in Serbian language is neuter, its gender in folklore is always male, as is the Moon's and the Wind's (see below). The Sun has a mother, the Moon is his brother and the Stars his sisters. In some parts, Venus is believed to be the Sun's wife.

3. In Serbian folklore, the Moon is a living being of male gender, like the Sun. He also has a mother, the Sun is his brother and his wife is either the Lightning or the Morning Star (Aurora). New Moon is believed to have healing powers, and people pray to it to give them health and happiness.

4. In Serbian folklore, the Wind is considered to be an important gift from God. If there was no Wind, spiders would weave their webs between the earth and the sky and people would not be able to survive. The Wind can be good or bad, bring rain or draught, heal or spread illness. It is believed the Wind comes from the ground, from underground caves or from the nostrils of a huge Aždaja fighting with the Sun (See also The Seven Little Vlachs).

5. Although this tale makes use of the motif of a childless woman giving birth to a non-human child, present in folklore of many different cultures (see Mr Peppercorn, Note 1), its main motif is that of an animal bridegroom, also widespread among various cultures. The Snake Bridegroom tale variants in particular can be found in the folklore of peoples and lands as diverse as the Zulu tribe in Africa, Jamaica and the West Indies, India, Burma, Russia and, of course, a number of European countries including Germany, Sweden and Denmark.

Tzar Trojan's Goat Ears

Once upon a time there lived a Tzar called Trojan. This Tzar, instead of human ears, had the ears of a goat. Whenever a barber was summoned to shave the Tzar's beard, the barber would never return home since, as soon as the shave was done, Tzar Trojan would ask the barber if he had noticed anything unusual about the Tzar's person. When the barber would say well, yes, he had seen the goat ears on the Tzar's head, the Tzar would reach for his sabre and cut the barber down on the spot. When it was this one particular barber's turn to go and shave the Tzar, he pretended he was sick, and so he sent his young apprentice in his stead. When the apprentice was brought to the Tzar, the Tzar asked him why his master wouldn't come, and the apprentice told him his master was ill. So the Tzar sat on a chair for the young apprentice to shave him. As the young man was shaving the Tzar, he noticed the goat ears on his head, but when the Tzar asked him if he had seen anything, the young man's response was no, he saw nothing at all. Then the Tzar gave him 12 dukats[1] and requested that it was always he who came to shave him from then on. When the apprentice returned home, the master asked him about his experience with the Tzar. The young man said that it was good, and how the Tzar had requested his services in the future, and he showed his master the 12 ducats, but he never mentioned the goat ears.

From then on, the young apprentice regularly went to shave the Tzar, and each time he shaved him he earned himself 12 ducats, and he never revealed to anybody that Tzar Trojan had ears of a goat. Eventually, however, the heavy burden of this secret began to wear him down, and he began to wither and wane. His master noticed this, and he asked the young apprentice what had befallen him. Upon the master's insistent questioning, the young man admitted how something was indeed bothering him, but that he could never reveal this to any living soul.

'If only I could tell somebody about it', he said, 'I would at once feel relieved'.

Then the master advised him thus:

'You can tell me about it, I will not pass it on to anybody else; if you feel wary of confiding in me, then go to a priest and tell him; if you feel wary of confiding in the priest, then go to the fields outside the city, dig a hole in the ground and lower your head into it, share your secret with the earth three times and then fill the hole again with soil.'

The young man listened to his master's advice and chose to follow the last of the three paths propounded. He walked far out into the fields beyond the city, dug a hole in the ground, lowered his head into it and proclaimed thrice:

'Tzar Trojan has goat ears!'

Then he filled the hole with soil again and, thus calmed and relieved of his secret burden, walked back home in peace.

When some time had passed, three beautiful, strong elder[2] saplings sprouted from the place where the young man had dug the hole and confessed his secret to the earth. Some shepherds then passed by this place and, spotting the beautiful saplings, cut one of them off and made a whistle. When they played the elder whistle, however, a voice came out of it and sang:

'Tzar Trojan has goat ears!'

In no time the word of this spread across the Tzar's city, and the Tzar himself heard the shepherds play:

'Tzar Trojan has goat ears!'

He then summoned the barber's apprentice, and demanded of him:

'Why on earth did you spread the word of my goat ears across the city?'

The young apprentice began assuring the Tzar how he never said a thing to any living soul, although he did indeed see what was on the Tzar's head. Tzar Trojan then reached for his sabre to cut the young man down, and the young man, overwhelmed with terror, confessed how he went out into the fields and dug a hole, and how later on elder tree saplings sprouted from the very same ground, and how any whistle made from this elder wood gave this voice out and spread the word of the Tzar's goat ears thus. The Tzar then demanded he be taken to the place where this elder grew to attest the truth of the young man's account. When they reached the place, they found only one of the saplings still growing from the ground, and the Tzar had a whistle made from this sapling. No sooner had his servants played this whistle, than a voice came out of it and sang:

'Tzar Trojan has goat ears!'

The Tzar then came to understand how no secret in this world could be kept forever, and how sooner or later, all things came to be known. So the Tzar pardoned the young man and from then on allowed any barber to come and shave him and to see his goat ears.

Notes

1. Ducat [**duhk**-uht], /ˈdʌkət/ is a gold coin produced and used for trade throughout Europe from the 12th century through until the early 20th century.

2. According to folklore, elder is a plant with magical properties, and its uses range from protection from evil forces through medical uses and relief of labour pains to the revelation of secrets. It is popular not only in Serbian and Slavic pagan mythology, but throughout Europe and the British Isles: Shakespeare's plays abound with mentions of elder trees and bushes, and it is the favourite wood for instrument making amongst the Faery folk and shepherds alike. Because of its strong pagan associations, Christian church tried to alter its image and to assign negative connotations to the plant, claiming that it was both the tree Judas Iscariot hanged himself from, and one of the trees that supplied the wood for the Crucifixion Cross, although the small size of the tree and its light weight would have made this highly unlikely, if not impossible.

PEPELJUGA

Once upon a time some maidens were grazing cows in a field. As they sat by a deep pit spinning yarn, an old man with a long white beard appeared and said to them:

'Maidens, you should take great care, for should one of you drop her spindle into the pit, her mother will instantly turn into a cow.'

And then the old man left. Mystified by his words, the maidens drew nearer the pit to take a peek inside, and one of them, the most beautiful one, dropped her spindle into it. When she got back home in the evening, she found her mother had turned into a cow and was standing in the yard outside. So she began taking this cow to graze with the rest of the herd.

When some time had passed, the maiden's father married a widow, who brought her only daughter with her. The stepmother hated her stepdaughter at first sight: the stepdaughter was far more beautiful than her own daughter. So she forbade her to wash her own face, brush her own hair or change her own clothes and kept looking for reasons to punish her. One morning she gave her a bag full of hemp and said:

'If you fail to spin all this today and roll onto a hank, do not come back home tonight, for I shall kill you.'

The poor maiden, as she grazed her herd, spun and spun the hemp. At midday, when the cows lay down in the shade, she began to weep, as it seemed like she had done no work at all—the bag of hemp looked just as full as it did in the beginning. Seeing her cry, the cow who was her mother asked her what had happened, and the maiden told her everything that had befallen her. The cow consoled her with these words:

'Weep no more and worry not. I shall chew the hemp and the thread will come out of my ear; take it as it comes out and roll it onto the hank.'

So they did; the cow chewed the hemp, and the maiden pulled the thread from her ear and rolled it onto the hank—in no time the job was done. In the evening, the maiden handed over the huge hank of thread to her stepmother; the woman was astonished to see this. The following day she gave the maiden an even bigger bag of hemp, and when the maiden brought back another huge hank of thread, the stepmother thought her friends must be helping her. So on the third morning she gave the maiden the biggest bag of hemp yet and sent her own daughter, by stealth, to go and see who was helping the maiden. Sneaking up, the stepsister saw the cow chewing the hemp and the maiden rolling the thread coming out of the cow's ear; she went back to her mother and reported this. The woman then asked her husband to slaughter the cow. The husband tried to dissuade her, but she kept insisting and demanding that the cow be slain, so the husband eventually gave in and set the day on which this was to take place. When the maiden found out about this, she began to weep inconsolably. The cow asked her why she was shedding tears, and when the maiden told her everything as it was, the cow said:

'Weep not, my daughter. When I am slain, do not eat any of my meat, but gather my bones and bury them under a certain stone in the yard; when you are in great need, come to my grave and you shall find help.'

When the cow was slaughtered and they began eating its meat, the maiden excused herself saying how she was not hungry and could not eat; instead she gathered the bones and buried them at the said spot in the yard. This maiden's name was Mara, but as she did most of the work around the house: fetched water, cooked food, washed up, cleaned the floors and did pretty much all the other household chores, including emptying the ash from the hearth, her stepmother and stepsister began calling her Pepeljuga[1].

One Sunday morning, the stepmother and her daughter went to church, and on their way out the woman scattered a bucketful of millet, saying to the maiden:

'Now, Pepeljugo, you shall gather this millet and prepare our lunch; should you fail to do this by the time we are back from the church, I shall kill you!'

As they left for the church, the maiden began to weep, saying to herself: 'Making lunch is easy, but how could I gather all this millet in time!?' Then she suddenly remembered the cow's words: when she gets in trouble, she should go to the cow's grave and she will be helped. The maiden rushed over to the grave and what was she to find there!—an open chest full of the finest dresses, with two white doves sitting atop it. The doves said to her:

'Maro, choose any dress from this chest, put it on and go to the church; we shall gather your millet and do everything else.'

Delighted, she took a dress made of the finest silk from the top of the pile, put it on and went to the church. When she arrived at the church, everyone was stunned by her beauty and by the beauty of her dress, and also by her mysterious appearance, since no-one knew who she was nor where she had come from. The Tzar's son who also happened to be present was the most astounded of them all.

Towards the end of the service, she sneaked out and ran back home. She took the dress off and changed back into her own clothes, and the chest closed by itself and disappeared from sight. The maiden then rushed back into the house; as she stepped in, she saw the millet all gathered and the lunch made and the whole house tidied up. Not long after, the stepmother and her daughter came back; they were astonished to find everything done as they had requested.

The following Sunday, the stepmother and her daughter again prepared to go to the church and on their way, the woman scattered even more millet over the floor, and ordered the maiden as before:

'Should you fail to gather all this millet, have everything cleaned and prepare lunch by the time we are back, I shall kill you!'

No sooner had they left, than the maiden ran over to the cow's grave. Once more, she found the open chest with dresses and the two doves atop it.

'Get dressed and go to the church, Maro,' they said. 'We shall gather the millet for you and do everything else as your stepmother requested.'

The maiden then took a dress from the top made of sterling silver, put it on and went to the church. Those gathered in the church were even more stunned by her beauty than on the previous occasion; the Tzar's son couldn't take his eyes off her. Towards the end of the service, she sneaked out again and rushed back home. She took the dress off and changed back into her own clothes, then went inside. When her stepmother and her daughter returned from the church, they were dumbfounded to find the millet gathered, the lunch made and everything else completed to their command; they couldn't comprehend how she could have done this.

So for the third Sunday in a row, the stepmother and her daughter got ready for church, and scattered an even bigger amount of millet on the way out.

'Should you fail to gather this millet, clean everything up and have our lunch made by the time we are back,' the woman said 'I shall kill you!'

No sooner had they left, than the maiden rushed over to the cow's grave once more; the open chest was there, and so were the two doves, telling her to get dressed and go, and they would do everything. The maiden picked a dress made of pure gold, put it on and went to the church. Once more, those gathered at the church admired greatly her beauty and her dress, and the Tzar's son decided not to let her out of his sight this time, but to follow her and see where she was going. Towards the end of the service, she sneaked out again to go back; but this time she lost one of her slippers and, not having the time to go back and get it, she ran off barefoot. The Tzar's son, who tried to follow her closely as she left, but could not squeeze past the crowd, saw her lose the slipper and picked it up. As she arrived back home, she did as before and changed back into her own clothes, then went to wait for her stepmother and stepsister.

The Tzar's son, slipper in hand, began searching for the maiden all over his Tzardom. He had each maiden try the slipper on for size; for some it was too long or too short, for others it was too narrow or too wide—none had the perfect fit. As he travelled from village to village, from town to town, he came upon the maiden's house. Seeing the Tzar's son approaching their house in search of the maiden from the church, the stepmother hid Mara under an upturned basin. When the Tzar's son walked in carrying the slipper and asked if they had a maiden in the house, the woman said yes and brought her daughter out. The Tzar's son had her try on the slipper, but she couldn't pull the slipper even half-way up her foot. The Tzar's son then asked if they had any other maidens in the house, and the woman said no. At that moment, a cock[2] leaped on top of the upturned basin and crowed:

'Cock-a-doodle-doo! She's under the basin!'

The stepmother yelled at the cock:

'Off with you, may an eagle snatch you!'

Hearing this, the Tzar's son rushed over to the upturned basin and lifted it up and what was he to find there!—the very same maiden he saw at the church, wearing the very same dress she had on the last time, her right foot missing a slipper. The Tzar's son was overcome with joy at this sight, and quickly slid the slipper on her right foot—it was a perfect fit in size and exactly the same as the slipper on her left foot! He then took her to his palace and married her.

Notes

1. Pepeljuga [pe-**pel**-yuga], /pe'peʎ,uga/ (from the Serbian word pepeo = ash) is the Serbian version of Cinderella—the name and the tale.

2. In Serbian folklore and Slavic mythology in general, a cock is a demonic animal, related to Svarog, a deity of the highest order in the Slavic mythological pantheon, the father of Dažbog (solar deity) and god of celestial light and of blacksmithing. It is believed that a cock has prophetic powers and can foresee weather changes, among other things.

The Seven Little Vlachs[1]

Once upon a time a realm was shared between two big Tzardoms: the Tzardom of Tzar Petar, and the Tzardom of Tzar Tatarin. Tzar Petar had a beautiful daughter, without a rival in the whole wide world. Tzar Tatarin wanted this maiden for his wife and he sent a message to Tzar Petar asking him to give his daughter's hand to him; should he refuse to do so, Tzar Tatarin would lead his army against Tzar Petar, burn, loot and conquer his Tzardom and take both him and his daughter captive. Having received this message, Tzar Petar said to the envoy:

'Go and tell your Tzar that my daughter has passed away, let him find himself another Tzaritza and drop this battle and war business.'

As soon as the envoy had left, Tzar Petar had a strong, solid tower built, big enough to hold two people and food and drink supplies sufficient for three years. When the tower was built, he went in with his daughter and built a wall over the entrance from inside. He entrusted his loyal servant with ruling the Tzardom in his absence for three years and when the three years had passed, the servant was to break into the tower and let him and his daughter out. He also ordered that they tell anyone who came looking for him that he had gone to the Sun Tzar to ask him why the days in the winter were not as long as the days in the summer and why they were so cold, preventing his subjects from doing much work and causing them to idle their time away.

Not long after, Tzar Tatarin came looking for Tzar Petar and his daughter. He was told that Tzar Petar's daughter had passed away and that the Tzar had gone to the Sun Tzar to ask him some questions. Tzar Tatarin entered the palace but seeing it empty of people and shrouded in deadly silence, he returned to his own Tzardom.

When three years had passed, the tower was broken into and Tzar Petar came ; his daughter was nowhere to be found. Tzar Petar himself hadn't a clue as to may have befallen her.

 day Tzar Petar left the tower, a death row prisoner was awaiting his execution. People flocked in their dozens to see the guilty man and he spoke to them thus:

'If only Tzar Petar knew, and he doesn't, that if he released me from prison and saved me from execution, I would find his daughter and bring her back to him.'

The prisoner's boasting words travelled fast and reached the Tzar himself. So he summoned the prisoner and asked him:

'Would you truly able to find my daughter and bring her back home, if I pardoned you and saved your life?'

And the prisoner replied:

'I would, if only I could be freed from these irons.'

Tzar Petar ordered that the iron ball and chains be taken off the prisoner, gave him some money for his journey and sent him into the world to look for his daughter.

The prisoner travelled the world far and wide asking after the Tzar's daughter, but no-one knew a thing about her. He went through nine different realms in this manner, and at the end of the ninth realm he came upon a house with an old woman inside.

'God help thee, mother,' he greeted her, stooping to kiss her hand.

'God help thee, my son! What brings you here?' she asked.

'I am looking for the daughter of Tzar Petar,' the prisoner replied.

He then told her all as it was, how she disappeared from the tower in such a way that not even her father, who was locked inside the tower with her, noticed her being taken; how he was a death row prisoner and had promised the Tzar he would find his daughter for him, should he pardon his crime; how he had passed through nine different Tzardoms already but the Tzar's daughter was nowhere to be found.

The old woman said:

'By good fortune, when you first saw me and greeted me, you called me mother and kissed my hand; by doing this you made yourself my son. I have five sons and each one of them is a Zmaj. Whenever they see a man in here, they tear him to pieces; I won't let them do this to you.'

Then she beckoned the prisoner to take a seat and began telling him:

'My first son is so stealthy, that he can take a live lamb from inside a live ewe without her even noticing. My second son is so skilled in following a scent and finding tracks, that he will discover them even if they are nine years old. My third son is such a skilled mason, that he is able to, in the blink of an eye, build a tall tower. My fourth son is so skilled with his bow and arrow, that he can shoot a star in the sky. And my fifth one is so skilled in catching things, that he can grab hold of thunder with his bare hands. And if they cannot find the Tzar's daughter and bring her back to you, no-one in this whole world can.'

No sooner did the mother of the Zmajs finish telling him this, than a howling came from outside: the five Zmajs, the old woman's sons, had returned. Quickly, the old woman hid the prisoner under a basin behind the door, so that her sons would not tear him to pieces at once, should they come back angry. They burst through the door and said:

'Good evening, mother.'

'Good evening, my children,' their mother replied. 'Welcome back! Have you had a nice wander?'

One of the sons replied:

'We have, mother.'

But the youngest son said:

'There is a human in here. Tell us, mother, where he is.'

'You are right, there is,' she said. 'Your brother-with-God is here. He made me his mother-with-God and I made him my son-with-God, since, as soon as he stepped in, he called me mother and kissed my hand.'

'And what is he after, this brother-with-God, in here?' the Zmaj asked.

'He's after the Tzar's daughter,' his mother replied. Then she recounted everything as she had heard from the prisoner and said:

'Tomorrow, my children, go out into the world and look for the Tzar's daughter. And now promise me you will not do a thing to harm your brother-with-God.'

They promised, and the old woman walked over to the basin, lifted it and let her son-with-God out; he greeted and embraced the Zmajs as his brothers. By the time all five of them finished hugging and kissing him, he had lost three ounces of blood.

After dinner, they went to sleep. The Zmajs and their mother, tired as they were, slept like babies; but the man could hardly sleep all night, since they had squeezed his body so hard when hugging him, he hurt all over.

The following day, at the crack of dawn, the Zmajs woke up and, taking their brother-with-God along with them, set off for the Tzardom of Tzar Petar. The Zmaj with the good nose smelled a scent on the road down which the Tzar's daughter had been taken. So they followed the scent all the way to the palace of a Zmaj with seven heads, who had, when her father was asleep in the tower, abducted the maiden so skilfully her father never sensed a thing.

Having discovered the Tzar's daughter's whereabouts, the Zmaj who was a skilled thief went inside the seven-headed Zmaj's palace and found him asleep on the maiden's lap. The stealthy Zmaj then took hold of the maiden and flew her out of the window so carefully and so quietly, the seven-headed Zmaj never felt a thing. When he awoke, however, he knew at once who had stolen his maiden and immediately gave chase.

The Zmaj who was a skilled mason spotted the seven-headed Zmaj chasing after his brother and the maiden and so he quickly built a tower for them all to hide inside. The seven-headed Zmaj flew over to the tower and shook his heads violently; three from right to left, three from left to right, and the seventh one in the middle up and down and began to spit fire. The sun then disappeared and darkness descended; you would have thought it was midnight, all of a sudden. In this darkness, the seven-headed Zmaj smashed the tower to smithereens, snatched the maiden and flew into the sky.

The Zmaj who was a skilled archer then shot an arrow into the sky and pierced the seven-headed Zmaj straight through the heart, so he dropped the maiden from his grasp. She began to fall towards the ground, and the seven-headed Zmaj followed.

Then the Zmaj who was skilled in catching things ran to catch the maiden in his arms and did this so gently she never felt a thing, and his brothers caught the seven-headed Zmaj in their arms and tore every one of his seven heads off before letting him drop on the ground.

And so the five Zmajs had rescued the Tzar's daughter. They were all delighted to have gained such a beautiful maiden and began to quarrel over who she belonged to.

The man interrupted their argument and said:

'Brothers, the maiden is mine. As you are very much aware, I must take her back to her father, in order to be pardoned and have my life saved. Had I not come searching for her, you would have never found her, since you never even knew she existed.'

The first Zmaj then said:

'The maiden is mine. Had I not found her, you would not have had her, so all your searching would have been in vain.'

But the second Zmaj said:

'The maiden is mine. Had I not managed to steal her from the seven-headed Zmaj, you would not have had her, and both your searching and your finding would have been in vain.'

The third Zmaj said:

'The maiden is mine. Had I not quickly built that tower for all of us to hide inside, the seven-headed Zmaj would have caught up with you and snatched the maiden away from you, so all your searching, finding and stealing would have been in vain.'

The fourth Zmaj said:

'The maiden is mine. Had I not shot the seven-headed Zmaj with my arrow, he would have taken her away again, and all your searching, finding, stealing and hiding would have been in vain.'

The fifth Zmaj said:

'The maiden is mine. Had I not caught her as she fell, she would have hit the ground and smashed to smithereens and you would not have had her; all your searching, finding, stealing, hiding and shooting would have been in vain.'

So they argued over who the maiden should go to, until they came upon the mother of the Wind and told her about their disagreement, asking her to give them their verdict and decide the outcome. Having heard all their arguments, the mother of the Wind asked:

'Have you been to the mother of the Moon and asked her to give you her verdict?'

'No, we have not,' they replied.

'Well then, you should go to the mother of the Moon; she will be able to give you a fairer verdict, since her son has been around for longer.'

The brothers and the maiden went to the mother of the Moon. Without even greeting her, they cried from her doorstep:

'The mother of the Wind sent us to you to decide who the maiden should go to!' Then they recounted to her everything as had happened, and each one of the brothers presented his argument for the maiden's hand.

The mother of the Moon asked:

'Have you been to see the mother of the Sun?'

'No, we haven't,' they replied.

'You should go to her, children,' she said. 'The mother of the Sun will be your fairest judge, since her son has seen the most of this world.'

So they went to the mother of the Sun. Without a greeting, they called to her from her doorstep:

'The mother of the Moon has sent us to you to decide who the maiden should go to.' Then they told her, too, all about their disagreement.

The mother of the Sun asked:

'Children, do you have a mother of your own?'

'We do, indeed,' they replied.

The mother of the Sun then sent them back home with these words:

'Go to your own mother, children. A mother is the best and the fairest judge of her own children. She will know best who the maiden should go to.'

So they returned home to their own mother and recounted everything that had happened, what each of them had done, where they had been, who they went to see and ask for counsel, and finally how the mother of the Sun had sent them back to her to give them fair verdict and decide who the maiden should go to.

Their mother said:

'Listen to your mother, my children. You are all my sons, so let the maiden be my daughter. You are all brothers; let her be your sister.'

The brothers were happy with this verdict.

108

All six brothers and their sister are now in the sky, and they are known as the Seven Little Vlachs. Each year they go to see the mother of the Wind, the mother of the Moon and the mother of the Sun to thank them for their advice. This journey lasts from St Đorđe's day[2] to St Vid's day[3], and during this time the Seven Little Vlachs cannot be seen in the sky.

Notes

1. Seven Little Vlachs are the Pleiades, or Seven Sisters—a cluster of stars of extraordinary beauty and brilliance, located in the constellation of Taurus. It is among the star clusters nearest to Earth and it is the most obvious one to the naked eye in the night sky. As such, it has provoked the human imagination since the beginnings of civilisation and numerous cultures have interpreted it in their own way over the millennia. The name Pleiades comes from Greek mythology, but evidence of its special place in folklore and mythology can be found all over the world: from the Berber people in the deserts of North Africa, to Middle Eastern cultures (it is mentioned in the Bible, the Islamic literature of Arabia and the Levant, Persia, Pakistan); from the various European peoples (Greek, Roman, Celtic, Slavic, Norse) to the indigenous peoples of the Americas; from Asia and Oceania (Aboriginal Australia, Japan, China, India, Indonesia, Polynesia, Thailand) to Sub-Saharan Africa. It continues to inspire the modern humankind, and many references can be found in popular culture, music and literature. The story here gives a typically Serbian take on the origin of the stars.

2. According to the Serbian Orthodox Church (which follows the Julian calendar), St Đorđe's (George's) day is celebrated on 6th May.

3. St Vid's (Vitus') day is celebrated on 28th June.

The Bird-Maiden

Once upon a time there lived a King and his only son. When the boy became a man and his time came to marry, the King sent him into the world to search for a wife. The King's son searched all over the great wide world but could not find a maiden for himself. Having wasted all this time and riches on his futile search, the Prince decided to take his own life and climbed up a steep hill, intent on throwing himself into the abyss. As he reached the top of the hill, he found a huge, solid rock protruding from the ground, stepped on it and was about to leap to his death, when he heard a voice behind him:

'Don't do it, young man, not for three hundred and sixty five days in the year!'

The Prince looked around and, seeing no-one, asked:

'Who's that talking to me? Come out into the open, and let me tell you my woes, for when you hear my woes, you will not mind me taking my own life.'

At that, a man appeared, with hair as white as a sheep, and spoke to him thus:

'I already know your woes; but can you see that big hill yonder?' And he pointed into the distance.

'I can', replied the Prince.

'And can you see yonder those many rocks?'

'I can.'

'Well, then,' said the white-haired man, 'atop yonder hill there is an old woman with golden hair[1], who sits on a spot day and night, holding a beautiful bird in her lap. He who gets hold of this bird, shall be the happiest man in the world; but be careful: you must, if you are brave and able enough, grab this old woman by the hair first, before she sees you, for if she sees you before you grab hold of her hair, you will be turned into a rock on the spot, like all those other young men standing there petrified, seemingly rocks and boulders.'

Hearing this, the Prince said to himself:

'I have no care and have nothing to lose, so I shall venture up that hill and, if I succeed in grabbing hold of her hairs before she sees me, I shall be fine; and if

110

not, I care not, for I am intent on taking my own life, anyway.' And so he climbe
the hill. When he was near the old woman, he sneaked up behind her and, as
luck would have it, at this moment the old woman was distractedly playing with
the bird in the sunshine and so, approaching her by stealth, he grabbed hold of
her hair. The old woman screamed so loud the whole hill shook as if from an
earthquake, but the Prince held tight onto her hair and would not let go. Then
the old woman said:

'What do you want from me?'

And the Prince replied:

'I want you to give me the bird from your lap and to bring back to life all these
Christian souls up here.'

The old woman agreed to this and gave him the bird, then breathed a kind
of blue air out of her mouth and towards the petrified men, and presently they
all came back to life. The King's son, taking hold of the bird, began to shower
her with kisses, filled with joy. From his kisses the bird turned into a beautiful
maiden. This maiden had been bewitched by the old woman and turned into a
bird to lure young men to their demise. Seeing the beautiful maiden, the Prince
felt like the happiest man in the world, and he decided to take her home with
him. As they started on their journey, the maiden gave him a staff, saying:

'This staff will do whatever you ask of it.' So the Prince tapped a rock with the
staff, and a load of golden coins burst out of the rock, enough to see him and the
maiden through their journey home. As they journeyed on, they came upon a
great big river, impossible to cross; so the Prince touched the waters with the staff
and the waters parted to open up a passage to the other bank. Further ahead, they
came upon a pack of wolves[2] that attacked them; but no sooner had a wolf come
near them, than the Prince laid his staff on it, and no sooner had he laid his staff
on a wolf, than it turned into an anthill. At long last, they reached the Prince's
home and they got married and they lived happily ever after.

Notes

1. According to Serbian folklore, a person's strength and might, as well as his or
her soul and destiny lie in the hair on their heads.

2. According to Serbian folklore, a wolf is a demonic animal; created by the Devil
himself, yet one that the Devil fears, too. One was advised to avoid saying its
name out loud, especially at night. If a wolf crossed one's path, it was considered
a bad omen. Simultaneously, accepting a wolf in one's family could protect the
family from evil spirits, as could naming a child 'Vuk'—wolf (like the given name
of the original collector of these tales).

Mr Peppercorn

Once upon a time there lived a woman who was barren[1]. This woman prayed to God day by day to let her have a child, even if it were as small as a peppercorn. Her wish was granted and she gave birth to a little boy, no bigger than a peppercorn. At first, she rejoiced so much at having born a child, she did not care it was so miniature in size; but as time went by and she watched other children, her son's peers, grow tall and old enough to marry whilst hers stayed as small as a peppercorn, she began to feel sad and to weep and lament daily.

One day she had a dream in which she was told to cry no more, as her son would grow as tall as a poplar tree. This dream made her happy, but her happiness was short-lived: her son came to tell her how he also had a dream, and that he must follow the path he was given in this dream. So he set out on his journey, leaving his crying mother behind.

Having travelled for some time, he came upon a Tzar's palace and walked into its garden. There he found the Tzar's daughter sitting under a tree, shedding tears. He bid her good day and asked why she was crying. She told him that the tree she was sitting under had born three golden apples and her father had sent her to keep watch over them; an Aždaja then came for three days in a row and took the apples one by one—the maiden was terrified of telling her father about this, since he had invited many a guest to come on the following day and see the gift God had given him. Mr Peppercorn told her to keep quite about it, and he would go find the Aždaja and bring the apples back to her, if she would kindly give him two of her servants to accompany him. He then bought a sheep and slaughtered it, quartered it and put all four shanks in his bag, throwing the rest away. He also took a length of rope and, joined by the Tzar's daughter's servants, went to the lake outside the city. There he tied the rope to a boulder and told the servants to lower him into the lake and when he tugged on the rope to pull him back out on to the ground. The servants did as he had asked and when he reached the bottom of the lake, what was he to find there—but a beautiful house with a garden. Inside the house he found the Aždaja sitting by the fire, cooking something in a cauld Seeing him enter, the Aždaja pounced on him to tear him apart, but he took of the sheep shanks out and threw it over to the monster. In the time the Ažda stooped to pick up the meat, he stole one of the apples. The Aždaja then pounce on him again, and he threw another sheep shank and stole another apple. Having devoured the meat, it then pounced on Mr Peppercorn once more, and he threw another sheep shank at it, thus stealing the third apple as well. When the Aždaja pounced on him for the fourth time, he threw the fourth cut of meat at it and made a dash for the exit; but just as he grabbed hold of the rope, the Aždaja came out the door and so he cut a piece of his own leg and threw it to the Aždaja. He then tugged on the rope and was pulled back out on to the ground. He took the apples to the Tzar's daughter and went on his way.

Not long after, the Aždaja took to going up to the Tzar's city every day and claiming a maiden as sacrifice. Eventually, the time came for the Tzar's daughter herself to be given as sacrifice to the Aždaja. At this point, the Tzar's daughter happened to be engaged, and her mother and father and her fiancé and all the noblemen accompanied her to the lakeside, hugged, kissed and said their goodbyes to her then left; her mother and father also turned to go back, weeping inconsolably, leaving her on her own to wait for the Aždaja. As she waited, she prayed to God to send Mr Peppercorn, who'd got the golden apples back from the Aždaja, to her rescue.

At that moment, Mr Peppercorn came back to the Tzar's city and, finding the place deep in mourning, he enquired what had happened. When they told him about the Aždaja and the sacrifices, he ran to the lakeside at once and found the Tzar's daughter there, sitting alone, shedding tears. He asked her if she would marry him, should he rescue her from the Aždaja.

'I would,' she replied. 'But you will not be able to rescue me; none could rescue me bar one, and he is not here.'

'And who would that be?' he enquired.

The Tzar's daughter replied:

'A man who, although he may be as tiny as a peppercorn, would no doubt be able to save me.'

Hearing this, Mr Peppercorn laughed and told her that it was him standing before her; he grew into a tall lad and had come to her rescue. She was astounded to hear this, but on his hand she saw the ring she had given him that time when he recovered the golden apples for her, and this reassured her it was, indeed, Mr Peppercorn himself standing before her. Then he asked her to let him rest his head on her lap for a little while and if he should doze off, to wake him when the lake began to shake. So he put his head in her lap and she began to stroke his hair; he fell asleep. All of a sudden, the lake began to shake and she shed a tear;

ear dropped on his cheek and he leaped to his feet, drew his sword and stood ·ing for the Aždaja.

Moments later, the Aždaja came out, with all its nine heads; it charged at him nd he cut one of the heads off; the Aždaja charged again, and he cut another one of its heads off, and so on until all the nine heads were gone. Mr Peppercorn than asked the maiden to give him a scarf, and he cut all the nine tongues from the nine heads off and wrapped them in the scarf; then, turning to leave, he asked the maiden not to tell anyone who came to her rescue, and he would yet come back for her when the time was right. And so he left.

On her way back, she came upon her fiancé who told her to say that he was the one who rescued her, and that if she wouldn't do this, he would kill her himself. The maiden pondered this for a little while then, remembering Mr Peppercorn's leaving words to her—how he would come back when the time was right, she promised to say that it was her fiancé who rescued her from the Aždaja. So the fiancé went back to the lake and collected all the nine heads for proof of his heroic deed.

When they returned to the palace, the maiden's parents were over the moon, they showered both her and her fiancé with kisses and hugs and decided to have them married at once, but the Tzar's daughter pretended she was sick in order to postpone the wedding day.

Several days later, Mr Peppercorn turned up and announced he was the one who rescued the Tzar's daughter. The Tzar did not know who to believe; his daughter was too frightened to say the truth as her fiancé had threatened to kill her if she did. So the Tzar ordered to have the matter settled in court; the one who could prove he rescued the maiden would have her for his wife. But when the fiancé showed the severed heads and Mr Peppercorn the tongues, the judge did not know who to believe, since the fiancé claimed he did not cut the heads off straight away but had run with the maiden back to her father first, and Mr Peppercorn showed them the maiden's scarf and said how she had dropped it in fear.

The Tzar then ordered them both to go to the church and pray the following day; the maiden was also going to be there and whoever got to the church first would have the maiden. Mr Peppercorn did not want to go before he heard the bells toll, but the fiancé rose in the middle of the night and went straight to the church. No sooner had he stepped one foot in it, however, than the ground opened and he fell through, into a pit full of blades. The maiden arrived shortly after and lit a candle, then sat by the pit to wait for the one she was destined to be with. As the bells tolled, Mr Peppercorn arrived. The Tzar then saw who was in the right, and had his daughter and Mr Peppercorn married. After this, Mr Peppercorn went to his mother so that she could see how tall a man he had become.

Notes

1. The motif of a childless woman who, after praying to God, gives birth to non-human child of unusal shape or size is fairly common in European folklore and can be found in the folk tales and folklore-based literature of many different nations; some examples include: *The History of Tom Thumb*—an English fairy tale; published in 1621, it was the first English fairy tale in print; *The Hazelnut Child*—a tale from the historic Central European region of Bukovina, 'the land of beech trees' (formerly an Austro-Hungarian duchy, currently part Romanian, part Ukranian); *The Goat Girl*—a Greek fairy tale; *The Myrtle*—an Italian literary fairy tale written by Giambattista Basile in his 17th century work The Pentamerone; *Hans my Hedgehog*—a German fairy tale collected by the Brothers Grimm and published in the 2nd volume of their Children's and Household Tales, a version of which was also produced as an episode of Jim Henson's televised series *The Storyteller*.

Once upon a time there lived a poor man in a cave. He had nothing save an only daughter, who was very wise and who went everywhere to earn a living for them with her words. She also taught her father how to speak well when asking for charity. One day, the poor man went to the Tzar's palace to ask for charity. Hearing him speak, the Tzar enquired where the man was from and where he had learnt to speak so well. The man told him where he was from and that it was his daughter who taught him wise words.

'And who taught your daughter?' the Tzar asked.

'God himself taught her, and our poverty,' the man replied.

The Tzar then gave the man thirty eggs and said:

'Take this to your daughter and tell her to have the chicks hatched from these eggs; I shall reward her handsomely for it. Should she fail to complete this task, however, you shall be faced with a great ordeal.'

The man took the eggs and went back to his cave in tears. He recounted everything the Tzar had said to his daughter. At a glance, the daughter realised the eggs were all boiled; she took them nonetheless and told her father not to worry, but to go and sleep, and she would have everything sorted out. Her father did as she asked and went to sleep. His daughter then put a big cauldron of water on the fire, and boiled some broad beans in it. In the morning, she said to her father:

'Go to the field with ploughshare and oxen, and plough the land by the road where the Tzar passes. When you see the Tzar coming, take these broad beans and shout:

"Now, oxen, with God's help, these boiled broad beans will grow!" When the Tzar asks how could boiled broad beans grow, you should tell him:

"Just as chicks can hatch from boiled eggs."'

The man listened to his daughter's instructions and went to plough the field by the side of the Tzar's road. Not long after, the Tzar appeared in the distance, and the man began shouting:

'Now, oxen, with God's help, these boiled broad beans will grow!'

Hearing this, the Tzar halted his carriage and asked:

'Poor man, how can boiled broad beans grow?'

And the man replied:

'Honourable Tzar, they can grow; just as chicks can hatch from boiled eggs.'

The Tzar at once understood that it was the man's wise daughter who taught him to say this. So he had the man brought to him; then gave him linseed yarn and said:

'Take this to your daughter and tell her to make out of it the sails, and ropes and everything else required for a ship; should she fail to complete this task, you shall be executed.'

The man was overcome with terror at hearing these words and he took the yarn back home to his daughter, sobbing all the way. When he told his daughter about the Tzar's latest request, she sent him to sleep again and promised she would have everything sorted out by the morning.

The next morning, she woke her father up holding a small piece of wood in her hands and she said:

'Take this piece of wood to the Tzar and ask him to have a loom, spindle, distaff and all other tools needed for weaving made from it, and I'll have the ship's sails and ropes done in no time.'

The man followed his daughter's advice and went to pass her message to the Tzar. The Tzar was astonished to hear this and began pondering what next to ask of this clever maiden. He then grabbed a tiny little cup and passed it to the father, saying:

'Take this cup to your daughter and tell her to take out all the water from the sea with it, so that it becomes a field.'

The man took the cup back to his daughter, crying. Having heard the Tzar's latest request, the daughter advised her father to go and rest and she would have everything sorted out over night. In the morning, she woke her father and gave him an ounce of mortar, saying:

'Take this to the Tzar and ask him to seal all the springs and all the lakes with it; and I shall have the sea emptied with the cup and turned into a field.'

The man did as she asked. When the Tzar saw that this maiden was far smarter than him, he had her summoned. Her father brought the maiden to the Tzar and the Tzar asked:

'Now tell me, maiden, what sound travels the farthest?'

The maiden replied:

'Honourable Tzar, the sound that travels the farthest is that of thunder and that of a lie.'

119

zar then held his beard and asked his attendants:

..ss how much my beard is worth?'

.ne said this much, other said that much, and the maiden said:

.ou are all wrong. The Tzar's beard is worth three Summer rains.'

.he Tzar was surprised with this answer and said:

'The maiden has got it right.'

Then the Tzar asked the maiden to marry him, saying that it had to be that way (she didn't really have a choice). The maiden curtsied and said:

'Honourable Tzar! Your wish is my command. I just ask you to write on a piece of paper, with your own hand, that should you ever feel angered by me and decide to send me away, I shall be allowed to take with me my most precious possession.'

The Tzar agreed to this and signed the paper.

When some time had passed, one day the Tzar got angry with his wife and said to her:

'I don't want you to be my wife any longer; leave my palace and go wherever you wish.'

His wife replied:

'Honourable Tzar, I shall abide by your words; just please let me stay the night in the palace and I shall be gone in the morning.'

The Tzar allowed her to stay the night in the palace. At dinner, she secretly mixed rakija and some herbs into his wine and, proffering the cup to him, said:

'Drink, my Tzar, and rejoice; for tomorrow we shall be parted, and trust my words: I shall be happier than when we first met.'

The Tzar drank and fell asleep. The Tzaritza put him in a carriage and took him to a cave. When the Tzar woke in the morning and found himself in a cave, he shouted:

'What on earth is this? Who brought me here?'

And the Tzaritza replied:

'I brought you here.'

'Why did you do this to me?' the Tzar asked. 'Haven't I told you that you are no longer my wife?'

The Tzaritza then took the paper out and showed it to the Tzar, saying:

'It is true, my Honourable Tzar, that you said I was no longer your wife; but look at this piece of paper: where you signed that I could take with me whatever I loved most in your home.'

Hearing this, the Tzar kissed the Tzaritza and together they returned to the palace.

THE VILA'S CARRIAGE

Once upon a time there lived a Tzar whose only daughter had never laughed in her entire life. This made the Tzar very sad, so he sent out word that he would give the hand of his daughter in marriage and half of his Tzardom to the man who succeeded in making his daughter laugh. In no time the word spread across the great wide world and thousands of the very best jokers and comedians from all parts gathered; alas, to no avail—none could make the Tzar's daughter laugh.

In a field close by, two women were reaping wheat, whilst a young man walked behind, tying the stalks into sheaves. They talked about the Tzar's challenge and the young man said to his mother:

'Mother, I shall go and make the Tzar's daughter laugh.'

His mother replied;

'Leave that nonsense be! Many a smarter man has tried already and had no success, and you think you can do better?!'

But the young man persevered and set off on his way. When he had walked for some while, a carriage came up behind him, with the sound of a flute being played coming from inside. As he turned to look he noticed the carriage was moving by itself—without any horses pulling it along—and inside it three maidens sat, one of whom was playing the flute.

He greeted them as they drew close:

'God help you, sisters-with-God!'

'God help thee, brother-with-God! Have you made us your sisters?' they asked.

'I have,' he replied. 'And have you made me your brother?'

'We have,' they replied—but unbeknownst to him, they were Vilas.

As they became siblings-with-God thus, the maidens stepped out of the carriage and said:

'Here's the carriage for you, and here's the flute; whichever direction you play the flute in, the carriage will follow, and when you stop playing the flute, the carriage will stop moving.'

121

ring this, he climbed into the carriage and began playing the flute; the
age began to move at once. In this manner he reached an inn, arriving just
ight began to fall. He drove the carriage into the courtyard and stopped there;
n walked into the inn and asked for food. After dinner, he went to sleep in
e carriage. The innkeeper had three daughters, and they had a habit of sleeping
n the nude. The young man's carriage had three golden apples sitting atop it; in
the darkness of the night, their lustre lit up the windows of the inn. The maidens
spotted the apples and decided to try and steal them from the young man. As
they thought, so they did; they went out into the courtyard and grabbed hold of
an apple each, but as they did this, their hands became glued to the apples. The
following morning, when the young man woke up he saw the naked maidens
stuck to the apples atop of his carriage; he cared little for this sight. He took his
flute out and began to play; the carriage began to move and the maidens hopped
alongside.

As they travelled thus, they came upon an army barracks, just as the soldiers
were cleaning their uniforms. Seeing the hopping naked maidens, they ran up
to them and grabbed hold of their breasts; their hands became glued to the
maidens' breasts and they too began hopping alongside the moving carriage and
the maidens. Our hero then turned to look, but still cared little for the sight; he
kept playing his flute and the carriage kept moving. When they were nearly at
the Tzar's palace, they passed by a house where a woman was baking bread in the
oven. When she saw the rabble round the carriage, she came out and struck one
of the soldiers over his back with her bread paddle; the paddle got stuck to his
back, and so did the woman.

And so they all arrived at the Tzar's palace. At the sight of this remarkable
scene, the Tzar's daughter began laughing uncontrollably from afar, and hearing
her laugh thus, her father the Tzar waved at the young man to stop the carriage.
He stopped the carriage and went before the Tzar.

'You made my daughter laugh,' the Tzar said, 'and she has never laughed before!
You shall have her hand in marriage.'

And so the Tzar had his daughter and our young man married, and the young
man was given half of the Tzardom to rule, which he is still doing, if he's still alive.

THE DARK REALM

Once upon a time a Tzar led his army on horseback to the end of the world and into the dark realm, where there was never any light and where darkness reigned. In order to find their way back from the darkness, the foals were left at the entrance so that the mares would lead the men back again into the light.[1] Entering the dark realm on foot, they felt some kind of small stones beneath their feet, and a voice came out of the darkness:

'Anyone who takes some of these stones with him will regret it, and anyone who does not will regret it, too!'

Hearing this, some of the men thought:

' Why should I take any, if I am going to regret it?'

And the others thought:

'I should take one, at least.'

When they returned to the light from the darkness, they found that the stones were all precious, and the ones who had not taken any stones with them regretted it, and those who had taken some—regretted not taking more.

Notes

1. Horses are intelligent and sensitive animals, able to find their way in night-time as in daylight. People always put their faith in horses to lead them safely to any destination. Led by her love for her foal, a mare would be able to find her way back even from the dark realm.

Index of Key Terms

Aždaja—a type of dragon; see The Young Tzarevich and the Aždaja, Note 5

Brother-with-God—blood bother; see The Golden Apple Tree and the Nine Peahens, Note 3

- **Vila**—a forest nymph; see The Maiden Who Was Faster Than a Horse, Note 1
- **Zmaj**—a type of dragon; see The Hovering Castle, Note 1

APPENDICES

Appendix 1: Serbian Alphabet

Serbian language is the only European language with active synchronic digraphia, i.e. it uses two different writing systems: Serbian (Vuk's) Cyrillic and Gaj's Latin alphabet. Serbian Cyrillic alphabet originated from two Slavic scripts, Glagolitic and Cyrillic, which were invented by the Byzantine Christian missionairies and brothers Ćirilo and Metodije (Cyril and Methodius) in the 860s; Vuk Stefanović Karadžić developed the modern Serbian Cyrillic in the early 1800s (see Introduction, Vuk Stefanović Karadžić). Gaj's Latin alphabet was devised by Croatian linguist Ljudevit Gaj in 1835, based on Jan Hus's Czech alphabet. Once there was a common language of the region, Serbo-Croatian, which used both alphabets; nowadays, the Croatian standard uses only Latin alphabet, whilst Serbian standard still uses both (although the Cyrillic alphabet has been the official script of the Republic of Serbia since 2006).

Cyrillic alphabet	Latin alphabet	IPA value
A a	A a	/a/
Б б	B b	/b/
В в	V v	/ʋ/
Г г	G g	/g/
Д д	D d	/d/
Ђ ђ	Đ đ	/dʑ/
E e	E e	/e/
Ж ж	Ž ž	/ʒ/
З з	Z z	/z/
И и	I i	/i/
Ј ј	J j	/j/
К к	K k	/k/
Л л	L l	/l/
Љ љ	Lj lj	/ʎ/
М м	M m	/m/
Н н	N n	/n/
Њ њ	Nj nj	/ɲ/
О о	O o	/ɔ/
П п	P p	/p/
Р р	R r	/r/
С с	S s	/s/
Т т	T t	/t/
Ћ ћ	Ć ć	/tɕ/
У у	U u	/u/
Ф ф	F f	/f/
Х х	H h	/x/
Ц ц	C c	/ts/
Ч ч	Č č	/tʃ/
Џ џ	Dž dž	/dʒ/
Ш ш	Š š	/ʃ/

Appendix 2: The Makers of This Book

Jelena Ćurčić
[**Yeh**-leh-nuh **Tchur**-chitch], /jelena tɕurtʃitɕ/

Jelena is a Writer, Translator and Storyteller; theatre-maker (Director/ Producer/Performer) and Applied Theatre Specialist (Community/Educational Settings, SEN). She has a theatre practice that works across formats and platforms, developing performance language in a manner highly engaged with audience and with community.

Born and brought up in Yugoslavia, she witnessed the violent, decade-long break-up of the country at the end of 20th century, actively participating in bringing about social change as a student of the **University of Belgrade**. After gaining her degree in English Language and Literature, she moved to London in 2002, where she worked for **The National Autistic Society**, teaching English and staging productions with young people on the Autistic Spectrum. In 2007, Jelena completed Directors' Apprenticeship at **The King's Head Theatre** and worked there for the remainder of the year as Assistant Director and, subsequently, Education Officer. In 2008, she founded **Flying Fish Theatriks**, an international artists' collective based at **Cable St Studios** in the East End of London (www. flying-fish.org). More recently, she has experimented directly with storytelling modes, making bespoke generative performances.

Jelena is an enterprising and tenacious individual, who is dedicated to the positive impact of the arts. In recent years she has been closely involved in the thriving arts culture at Cable Street Studios, helping manage the **Playhouse** venue, coordinating events and staging the monthly night of spoken word and alternative comedy, **A Night of Cock & Bull**. This has been the setting for Jelena's intimate storytelling project: **Four Seasons Story-Box: *Portals, Microcosms and The Art of Storytelling***, a series of 10-minute stories performed in monthly instalments, for two members of the audience at a time.

Besides her theatre practice and extensive work as a theatre-maker (Writer/ Director/ Producer/ Performer), she also regularly works as a Translator: most notable credits include Milan Marković's play ***Good Morning, Mr Rabbit***, which she translated and directed for Flying Fish's East London Tour in 2008/09 and ***Buried Land***, by Steven Eastwood and Geoffrey Alan Rhodes, a feature film produced in the Bosnian Valley of the Pyramids in Visoko, Bosnia, September 2008 (Official selection: Tribeca, Moscow, Mumbai, Sarajevo, Goteborg; East End Film Festival 2011)—Jelena worked as a Production Assistant and Head

...slator on the feature during 2009/10.

Jelena lives and works in London, UK.

Theatre credits include:

The Cable St Conundrum (site-specific), Original Concept, Director, Cable St Studios, (June 2009)

Milan Marković's ***Good Morning, Mr Rabbit***, Director, People Show Studios and East London Tour (January 2009—March 2009)

American Shorts, Co-Director with Ellie Joseph, featuring short plays by David Ives, Nina Shengold and Carol Real, King's Head Theatre, (October 2007)

Jorg Tittel's ***2+2+2***, Assistant Director/ Movement Coach, King's Head Theatre, (July 2007)

Serbian Fairy Tales is Jelena's first published book.

www.rosannamorris.com

Rosanna Morris

Originally from Bristol, illustrator Rosanna Morris spent her childh.. exploring the idyllic Somerset countryside and drawing inspiration fr nostalgic themes and humble lives, folklore, herbs and chickens. She gained h Foundation Arts Degree at **Bristol School of Art** in 2010 (Distinction), followe. by a BA in Illustration at **Camberwell College of Arts, University of the Arts, London**, in 2012.

Rosanna's work explores form with a linear approach, combined with eclectic smudges of watercolour. She is interested in people, their characters and idiosyncrasies, with reference drawn from film and a large archive of historic photographs.

Exhibitions:

Coop Project, (group show) Camberwell Gallery, London, June 2011
Slander and Libel, (group show) The Crypt, London, May 2010

Published Work / Commissions:

Cards—a set of two English woodland fauna cards, September 2011

Rye Lane - published newspaper illustrating Peckham, London, October 2011

Artisan Roast—10 separate illustrations designed for coffee bags, November 2011

Jeeves and Jemima Household services—8 separate illustrations used for website and branding. February 2012

Milliner—10 separate illustrations for website and branding, February 2012

Bibliography/ References

ɔseph Campbell, *The Hero With a Thousand Faces*, Novato, California: w World Library, 2008

2. Antti Aarne, *The Types of the Folk-tale: A Classification and Bibliography*, Suomalainen Tiedeakatemia, 1987

3. Stith Thompson, *Motif-Index of Folk-Literature: A Classification of Narrative Elements in Folk Tales, Ballads, Myths, Fables, Mediaeval Romances, Exempla, Fabliaux, Jest-Books, and Local Legend*, Indiana University Press, 1989

4. Meša Selimović, *Za i protiv Vuka*, BIGZ, Beograd, 1987

5. *Misterije Srbije*, RTS, 2007

Acknowledgements

The making of the Serbian Fairy Tales project as a whole and this bc
particular has depended on numerous participants, partners and suppor
First and foremost, two key organisations:

Arts Council England and **Serbian Council of Great Britain**, without whose
support this ambitious work would not have been possible.

Serbian Society, The Embassy of the Republic of Serbia in London and Serbian
City Club have also supported the project.

The following individuals have provided a significant contribution, either
morally and practically, with advice and guidance, or with financial support
(and, in many cases, in more than one way);

ETERNAL GRATITUDE TO YOU ALL:

The Ćurčić family: Snežana, Stojana, Smiljana, Nevena, Manojlo and Đorđe;
Dennis Patrick Bugler; The Hartley family: Glenn, Lize-Marie and Elizabeth;
Steve Harris; Sarah Sanders; Kristine Kilty and Richard Stott; Lorenzo
Sprengher; Sam Quinn; Paul Garayo; Ewan Bleach; Marie Bourel; Stuart Ekers;
Sarah Doody; Virginia Pontiveros Calzado; Becky McGahern; Cathy Rowsome;
Zio; Maya Jordan; Miki Stojiljković; Charlie Nikolić; Đorđe Nikolić; Avram
Balabanović; Rebecca Beaconsfiled; I S and N Banašević; Jadranka Đurđević;
Željana Grabovac; Natasha Koscis; Jelena and Daniel Kržanicki; Vesna Petković;
S Popović-Ward; Pru Porretta; Nina Rukvić; Stan Smiljanić; Mirjana Šijan;
Dušan Sofranac; M Stanojević; Olga Stanojlović; Sherly Stainly; Sanja Stojanović;
Slavica Stojsavljević; Branco Stoysin; Željko Vraneš; Thirere Hull; Jacqueline
Anda; Jelena Gerreyn.